Sonora Taylor

RAW DOG
SCREAMING
PRESS

Errant Roots © 2024 by Sonora Taylor

Published by Raw Dog Screaming Press
Bowie, MD

First Edition

Cover art copyright 2024 by Lynne Hansen
LynneHansenArt.com

Printed in the United States of America

ISBN: 978-1-947879-79-9
Library of Congress Control Number: 2024944460

RawDogScreaming.com

Also by Sonora Taylor

The Crow's Gift and Other Tales

Please Give

Wither and Other Stories

Without Condition

Little Paranoias: Stories

Seeing Things

Someone to Share My Nightmares: Stories

Diet Riot: A Fatterpunk Anthology (with Nico Bell)

Recreational Panic: Stories

For my mother and my mother's mother.

Acknowledgments

I'd like to thank R.J. Joseph and Jennifer Barnes for accepting my manuscript for publication. I'd also like to thank Joseph, Barnes, and Stephanie Pearre for their edits. Finally, I want to thank Evelyn Duffy, who gave the manuscript a first pass before I submitted it. All of these people helped bring the story to life.

I want to thank Laurel Hightower, who read an early draft and gave me the confidence to think I had something with this story.

There are so many wonderful people in the horror community that to name them would fill an entire book. A few I want to name and thank, though, are V. Castro, Gemma Amor, Todd Kiesling, Red Lagoe, Tiffany Michelle Brown, Ronald Kelly, Steve Stred, Erin Sweet al-Mehairi, and Brian Keene. Thank you all for your friendship, encouragement, and talent.

Thanks to my parents for their unwavering love and support.

Finally, thanks to my husband, Will; who gives me more strength than he'll ever know.

Content warnings can be found on the last page of this book.

ERRANT ROOTS

Horticulture

Family matters matter more than most believe. That's not to say that people don't value the roots and branches that snake their way from life to life, but rather that they underestimate the intractability of these structures.

They pull as tightly as they bind, these chains of blood. We can stay, or run, or hide, but any action we take is in response to these connections. Blood is memory, and our memory and the memory of us—be it trauma, triumph, or that strange place in between—is the collective sum of who we are.

Without our family, there is no us. But what then, when family becomes a plague? A terror one can only hope to someday escape? Is such a thing possible when errant roots may yet still linger?

It is sweet serendipity indeed that this next SPECSAP entry—to coin the phrase of my twin and colleague, [REDACTED]—is titled as such. Sonora Taylor's *Errant Roots* is an exploration of twisted family values, and the ties that band each generation to the next. But also how these offshoots continue to grow, even when those involved aren't aware.

My two predecessors in these introductions both relate things to memory, and as such, I shall continue to do so. Memory serves as an influence in this tale, a drive to follow tradition whether one agrees with it or not. Harriet can't help but take Deirdre back to a place of suffering due to the lingering effects of the cult-like family she grew up in, despite the fact that she left in the first place. Like Maxine's mother and father in *Hollow Tongue*, this programming—this memory of her time before—haunts her, even from a distance, growing more powerful with proximity. But in this work, the narrative lies in the coming generations: Deirdre and her cousins, caught up in this web of ritual murder led by the matriarch of their family.

Proof that even spilled blood can still bind people together, it would seem. I ask again, whether or not one can escape the memory—the tangled branches—of family.

You'll have to read to find out. My work deals with the past, not spoiling the future.

Errant Roots may bear strange fruits, and none can know what will be left after the harvest until it is upon them. Step into this tale that tracks the family tree of Deirdre and Harriet in this exquisite exploration of familial bonds and the knives that threaten to rend them apart, to see what unfolds.

Penned by the hand of [Redacted],
Head Genealogist and Ancestral Researcher

Chapter 1

"Do you know why ghosts float, Harriet?"

Harriet held her mother's hand as they walked through the woods behind their house. Despite the darkness, her mother used only the moonlight and a well-trodden path to guide them. They walked barefoot, and with every step, Harriet felt a burst of cold from the fallen leaves and scattered grasses like a heavy sigh upon her feet.

"It's because of our muscles." Her mother stooped down and tickled the underside of Harriet's foot. Harriet jumped back with a squeal of delight. "I just tickled your skin and your muscles. I didn't touch the bone."

"You didn't?" Harriet stopped and lifted her foot to examine it.

"Nope." Her mother set down her mallet and bent to Harriet's eye level. "Put your foot down." Harriet did as she was told. Her mother traced her finger over Harriet's foot in the shape of a pitchfork. "Your bones are right here. Resting on top of the muscles and skin. Walking on their own little pillow to protect themselves."

"Wow," Harriet breathed. Her mother picked the mallet back up and stood, holding out her free hand so Harriet could take it. They continued along the path.

"When we die, we become memories," she said. "And sometimes those memories manifest into spirits. Ghosts remember walking, and their bones remember walking above the ground. So their spirits float above the ground, reconciling their lost bodies."

"What does reconcile mean?"

"It's making up for things that are missing." They braced against a sudden gust of wind. Harriet wished she were back at the bonfire with her aunt and her sisters.

"Come on, honey," her mother said as she moved them both forward. "The sooner we finish, the sooner we can go back to the fire."

Harriet marveled at how her mother could read her mind. She'd asked her once if she could, and her mother replied, "Enough that if you even think about causing me trouble, you better think twice." Harriet minded her thoughts as best as she could after that.

They soon approached a clearing, where Harriet saw two feet pointed upwards in the moonlight. Once the wind settled, she heard the soft moan of her Uncle Max, although he wasn't moving.

"We've scattered a lot of seeds on this property," Harriet's mother said as she moved to Uncle Max's right side. "No," she said when Harriet followed her. "Stand across from me."

"Please," Uncle Max breathed.

Harriet looked down at his bruised face and bleeding chest. She wondered why he wasn't dead, but knew he would be soon. Otherwise, the seeds wouldn't scatter and their family would end.

"Those seeds carry ghosts, ones that whisper in our ears to disturb the branches. Your Meemaw says we need to tend to the bodies." Her mother knelt down, and Harriet followed. Her mother fished inside the pocket of her cardigan, then produced two gleaming, large nails. She held out the nails towards Harriet. "We need to secure his ghost."

Harriet took a nail from her mother's outstretched palm. Her mother handed her the mallet. The nail was heavy, but the mallet almost brought her hand down.

"Remember," her mother said, "fast and driving, like we practiced with the wood. Use your might."

Harriet ignored her uncle's dying whimpers as she placed the nail over his foot. She thought of the bonfire, of Constance and Patience dancing with her grandmother and Aunt Sarah. She wondered if Aunt Sarah had stopped crying yet.

Harriet raised the mallet and took a deep breath. She swung the mallet down with all her might. It clanged against the nail, its thunk vibrating through her skin.

Uncle Max's scream tore through the woods. Harriet looked at her mother. Her mother looked at her with pride, pride that filled Harriet's heart every time she saw it. She'd do anything her mother asked.

Chapter 2

Deirdre Croft rubbed her stomach as she ate her fourth plate of bumps on a log in one day. She wondered if the baby she carried was part elephant, given their apparent fondness for peanut butter. Deirdre had gone through almost two jars a week for the past month, the craving near-insatiable.

Be it peanut butter or anything else, Deirdre was ready to give her all to her daughter. Or maybe her son—she didn't know the baby's sex yet. Deirdre had a feeling, though, that she was having a girl. When she imagined the baby outside of her womb, she felt a feminine energy surrounding the image of a smiling child in her arms.

It may have been wishful thinking as opposed to intuition, but then again, her mother always told her to trust her intuition. "Even when it takes you places you're not sure of," her mother told her when Deirdre had first started sharing her doubts with her at a young age. "Especially then. That can be the hardest time to follow your intuition, but also the most necessary."

Though her mother hadn't confirmed it then, Deirdre had figured she was alluding to her own frayed relationship with her

14

family. Deirdre had never met a single one of her grandparents, nor any aunts, uncles, or cousins. She was an only child, and she'd never met her father—her mother told her he'd died before she was born. Whenever her friends at school talked about large family gatherings filled to the brim with cousins and second cousins, great-grandparents, and uncles twice removed, she'd wonder how on earth so many people could make someone feel at home or feel like family. As long as she'd been alive, it'd been her and her mother; and that was more than enough.

Now, though, a baby was going to be added to their duo— something Deirdre hadn't planned at all. She still remembered the day she found out, how she'd cried over three pregnancy tests with the tell-tale lines staring up at her. The only thing that interrupted her sorrow was a text from her mother letting her know that she'd arrived at the café where they'd been meeting weekly for coffee and conversation since she'd moved out after college. Deirdre thought about canceling, then decided against it. Something told her to share this with her mother, that her mother would know what to do.

"Deirdre!"

Deirdre looked and saw her mother waving at her from their usual table. Deirdre wondered how much longer her mother would have the huge smile she wore as she stood up to greet her with a hug.

"How are you, honey?" her mother asked as she pulled her close.

"I'm pregnant," Deirdre blurted.

Her mother stepped back with widened eyes. Deirdre looked down at the table, where their usual order waited for them—two vanilla lattes, whole milk.

"Pregnant?" her mother asked.

Deirdre nodded. Her mother stepped back and looked away from Deirdre. Her eyes went to some distance that Deirdre couldn't see, one probably filled with sorry thoughts about her disappointing, knocked-up daughter. She swallowed back the lump forming in her throat and squeezed her eyes shut.

"Oh honey," her mother said. "Don't cry, it's okay."

"I'm sorry."

"Sorry? Why are you sorry?"

"I don't know!" Deirdre wiped away a tear as they each took their seats. "I feel like I fucked up somehow."

"It's Tom's, right?"

"Of course!" Deirdre picked up her latte in irritation, then slammed it back down when she remembered she probably shouldn't drink coffee. "I'm not sleeping around."

"I didn't say you were," her mother said.

"But I'd be a fuck-up if I was, right?"

"Deirdre." Her mother took her hand. While the touch was tender, the look in her eyes told Deirdre to cut it out—now. It was a look she was familiar with, and even at twenty-four, it worked.

"I'm saying no such thing. It was simply a question—perhaps a shortsighted one, but nothing accusatory. I'm not mad at you. The only one mad at you is yourself."

Deirdre took a deep breath, then nodded. "Tom and I weren't planning this—obviously," Deirdre continued.

"Looks like something else planned it, though."

Deirdre snorted as she reached for her coffee, then clenched her fingers to stop herself. "Here," her mother said, switching their cups. "Mine's decaf today."

"There's a time and a place for decaf," Deirdre said with a smile as she took it. "Never, and in the trash."

"Well, pregnancy can change hard-held beliefs," her mother replied as she sipped Deirdre's drink.

Deirdre sighed and leaned back against her chair. "What am I going to do, Mom?"

"We'll see this through together, that's what."

"Even if Tom's not in the picture?"

Her mother set down her drink. "Did Tom leave?"

"Tom doesn't know. I just found out this morning."

"Tell him."

"But –"

"He should know. He should be there."

"I wasn't planning on marrying him or anything. We were dating and having fun, seeing where things would go."

"They went to a baby. Maybe the baby is showing you where your future lies with him."

"Harriet!"

Both Deirdre and her mother looked up and saw a barista holding up a steaming panini. "One chicken caprese for Harriet!" they called out.

"That's my lunch," her mother said as she got up.

Deirdre sat with her mother's words as Harriet got her sandwich. She hadn't been thinking of a long-term future with Tom, but she also hadn't been planning to break up with him anytime soon. She'd liked where they were going. Imagining him by her side with a baby, helping her feed the baby and change their diapers, wasn't the worst thought in the world.

"You don't seem as upset as you were before," her mother observed when she sat back down.

Deirdre smiled a little. "I was thinking about the future. About what it'd be like with me, Tom, and a baby. It … it wasn't so bad."

Harriet smiled. "It's meant to be."

After Deirdre told her she was pregnant, Harriet started to talk about introducing Deirdre to the rest of her family. It started quietly at first, a passing reference to the child's great-grandmother, or her mother talking about growing up with her sisters and wondering about their own children. "You have two cousins, last I heard," her mother told her at another café date.

"How do you know?" Deirdre asked. "I thought you hadn't spoken to them in years."

"I got back in touch recently."

"Why?"

"Why do you think?" Her mother nodded towards Deirdre's stomach. Deirdre felt oddly defensive of the child growing inside of her.

"It couldn't hurt to let them know we have a new member of the family on the way," her mother continued. "Or to introduce the baby to a few more relatives."

"You never wanted to talk to them before. Why does your grandchild suddenly get all these relatives?"

"When you get older, Deirdre," —Deirdre rolled her eyes. She hated it when her mother said her name to patronize her—"you'll find yourself wanting to nourish the roots linking you to your family tree. Not severing them."

"Hard for me to say. I've never met anyone else in our family except you." *And that's enough for me,* Deirdre added in her thoughts.

Harriet's talk of her family grew along with Deirdre's belly. It culminated at a dinner that her mother invited both Deirdre and Tom to. Deirdre thought that it was a simple get-together, a way for the three of them to spend more time together now that Tom was going to be a more permanent fixture in their lives. Her mother, though, pulled that rug from under their feet the moment the waiter took their orders.

"Mama wants to meet you," her mother said. "She wants to meet you both. They all do."

"All of them?" Deirdre asked.

"Yes. Mama, Constance, Patience—"

"Constance and Patience?"

"My sisters."

Deirdre smirked. "Pretty old-fashioned. Were you Amish?"

"No. Not all the names are so old-fashioned—your grandmother's name is Yvonne."

Deirdre dropped her smile when her mother didn't laugh. Harriet seemed only serious when discussing her relatives—serious, reverent, and perhaps a little fearful. It was something Deirdre had trouble reconciling with the fact that Harriet seemed determined to introduce them into her life. Why did they matter now—and why did they matter at all if Harriet was afraid of them?

"Makes sense to me they'd want to meet you," Tom said, easing any tension that had started to settle on Deirdre's shoulders.

"They do," her mother added, "as do my aunt and nieces."

"How many relatives do you have?" Deirdre asked, hoping the number of relatives suddenly entering her life wouldn't become out of control.

"Just those."

"Anything else I should know about them?"

"Well, my sisters and I are triplets."

"Excuse me?" Deirdre tried to imagine three carbon copies of her mother wandering around town.

"Not identical. Well, my sisters are identical twins. I was the extra that floated on in. At least that's what Mama always said." Harriet laughed, but it sounded sad. Pity entered Deidre's heart. She'd never considered how hard it must have been for her mother to leave the people she'd grown up with behind, to watch her child grow and not share it with her own mother.

Deirdre thought of these phantom relatives, ghosts floating into her mind that all looked a little like her mother. They wandered the sidewalks and entered her home, laughed over dinner, and cooed over her growing belly. Maybe getting to know them now would be a good thing.

"Well, maybe we can invite them all to the baby shower," Tom offered.

"I was thinking a gender reveal party," her mother said.

Tom and Deirdre both furrowed their brows. "Aren't those kind of outdated?" Tom asked.

"It's not unusual to find out the gender," her mother replied.

"The sex," Deirdre corrected.

"Either way, it's something my family would love to be a part of. They've never had one like you see on the Internet now."

"I'm not handling any explosives that'll make Deirdre a single mom," Tom cracked.

"Nothing like that," Harriet said with a laugh. "But maybe popped balloons, or one of those gender reveal cakes like you see on TV that—"

"Tell whether it's a boy or a girl with the color, yeah," Deirdre said. "Chandra makes those all the time."

"You could order one from her, maybe get a discount."

"So we have a party and invite everyone," Tom said.

"Not everyone," Harriet said. "I was thinking this could just be with my family, a way for Deirdre to get to know them without a bunch of hubbub from other people."

"So I'd be the only one going to this party?" Deirdre asked.

"No, Tom should come too."

"Why should Tom come if his parents and our friends can't be there?"

"I don't mind," Tom said curtly, "if you want me to be there, that is."

"Of course I do," Deirdre said. She squeezed Tom's knee under the table in an effort to quell any growing tension between them. She didn't want to argue with him about his feeling left out—not now.

"So it's settled," Harriet said as she flicked her napkin over her lap as if her daughter and her daughter's boyfriend weren't sitting with pursed lips on the verge of an argument. "We do the gender reveal at my mother's."

Tom looked at Deirdre, unwilling to answer himself. Deirdre folded her hands under her chin, then after a moment, nodded.

Now Deirdre sat in her kitchen, licking peanut butter off her fingertips and thinking of the family she'd never met. She looked at the white box on the kitchen table, which held a gender reveal cake from Chandra. Neither Tom nor Deirdre knew what color the cake was, blue or pink; though whenever Deirdre imagined slicing into it, she only saw pink crumbs tumbling onto her imaginary plate.

"Ready for the big reveal tomorrow?"

Tom broke through Deirdre's thoughts as he walked into the kitchen. He kissed her cheek as he sat down next to her.

"I guess," Deirdre replied, her thoughts about meeting her relatives still taking up space in her mind.

"You don't sound very excited, considering this was you and your mother's idea."

"It was all Mom's. You know that."

"You agreed to it."

"Can we please not argue about this? You know I feel bad about this just being our side of the family." They'd had a big argument about it after their dinner with Harriet, though once the argument became crying and apologies, it concluded with some of the best sex Deirdre had ever had.

"We can only argue about it if we have that kind of post-fight sex again," Tom joked. Deirdre laughed, and the tension between them disappeared faster than Deirdre's snack from her plate.

"Deal."

"Seriously though, what's wrong?" Tom nodded towards the cake box. "Worried it'll be a boy?"

"I'm not even thinking about that, really—well, maybe a little. And I'd be happy no matter the sex."

"Then what's got you so unhappy now?"

Deirdre sighed. On the one hand, it was comforting to have someone like Tom who always asked what was wrong and tried to fix it, be it with his humor or with a listening ear. On the other hand, it still unnerved Deirdre to have someone in her life that she couldn't hide anything from, even if she wanted to. Her mother often knew how she was feeling even when Deirdre did her best to keep those feelings away from her. Tom could see right through her too, but as they'd grown closer, Deirdre felt her resolve to keep some things to herself diminishing—something she didn't altogether mind, and something that told her she was truly in love.

"I wouldn't call it unhappy," Deirdre said. "Maybe nervous. Or trepidatious."

"About meeting all these new people?"

"All of them. All at once! Why are all these people suddenly so important to Mom? Why didn't she introduce me to them at my college graduation? My sweet sixteen, my thirteenth birthday? Why not any birthdays, or Christmases, or Thanksgivings? Why now? Why"—Deirdre ran her free hand over her stomach—"this?"

"Usually weddings and funerals bring families together. We're not getting married yet, and maybe she figured a baby is a happier occasion than a funeral."

"It's just so unlike her. Whenever I'd ask about any family members when I was younger, she'd barely talk about them. She'd say *we* were a family, me and her. She said that was enough. Now she talks about her mother and her sisters like they're a missing piece she isn't complete without."

"Your guess is as good as mine. I don't know what her reasons are beyond what she's told us, which is that she wants us—wants you, especially—to get to know your relatives now that there's a new member of the family on the way. It doesn't mean that all her talk about just you and her being family was a lie. It simply means there are more puzzle pieces. Or more fruit in the bowl. Or—"

"You can stop. I know metaphors aren't always your strong suit."

"Well, I hope you'll stop worrying so much about these relatives. You've never met them and haven't heard a thing about them until these past couple months. Why assume that there's something amiss?"

Because it was something Deirdre could feel in her gut, a tiny worm that burrowed deeper with each moment. Deirdre couldn't ignore her intuition. Her mother had raised her to trust it.

Now, though, Harriet had decided for Deirdre. She'd told her to not be so nervous, that there was nothing to worry about with this reunion. Deirdre expected that of Tom—men couldn't help themselves from explaining away women's feelings—but Deirdre expected more from her mother. Harriet was backtracking on how she'd raised Deirdre because Deirdre was acting in ways that weren't complicit or in agreement with her.

Deirdre could feel tension between her eyebrows and an increased clench in her jaw. She relaxed. She didn't want to share these feelings with Tom or with Harriet. They wouldn't listen anyway, and in a way, it comforted Deirdre to know she was still capable of keeping something to herself.

"I shouldn't assume," Deirdre said. She gave Tom a kiss. "Come on, let's enjoy some alone time before tomorrow."

Tom kissed her back—deeply, and with his tongue. "Maybe some sex without the arguing beforehand?" he said with a smile against her lips.

Deidre chuckled as she ran her hand up his leg. "You've got it."

Chapter 3

Deirdre held the cake in her lap as her mother drove her and Tom down roads increasingly lined with trees as opposed to buildings. They were changing with the season, and flecks of orange, yellow, and red swirled from the branches as they sped along. They'd gotten up so early that Deirdre wished more than ever she was allowed to drink coffee.

"We have a long drive ahead of us," Harriet had said in greeting as she and Tom got into her car. "Even without all the bathroom breaks you're going to need."

"Why can't we just drive ourselves then, so you can get there at the crack of dawn and we can be fashionably late?"

"It's easy to get lost on the way, and the GPS signal will knock out before we get there."

Their conversation stayed sparse, mostly due to how tired Tom and Deirdre were. Harriet seemed content to listen to the radio and play the silent chauffeur. As Deirdre moved in and out of dozing, she watched the sky grow brighter and the trees grow fewer.

"How long's it been since you've been back?" Deirdre asked.

Her mother stayed quiet for several moments. Deirdre glanced at her just as she answered, "A long time."

"How long?"

Silence again. Deirdre rolled her eyes and was about to look back out the window when her mother answered, "Twenty-four years."

"Wow, that's—" The number settled onto Deirdre's brain like the yellow leaves currently dotting the empty road ahead of them. "That's my age."

"I left when I was pregnant with you."

"Were they mad you got pregnant out of wedlock or something?"

"No. Your grandmother was thrilled, really. Another baby. Another girl."

A snore from Tom cut them off. Deirdre looked in the rearview mirror and saw him passed out against the window.

"Your grandmother has a thing with numbers," her mother continued, which brought Deirdre's attention back. "I was also twenty-four when I was pregnant with you. And your grandmother was forty-eight when I was pregnant, just like I am now. And my grandma was seventy-two. See a pattern?"

Deirdre considered the numbers, then smiled. "*The Days of the Croft Family*," she said with the flourish of a soap opera announcer.

"That's right." Harriet chuckled, and Deirdre was happy to see her smile. "She saw our lineage as a cycle, one with a perfect sunrise and sunset. Days that pass through the womb."

Deirdre had to admire the prettiness of that thought, even if their ages had no more significance than that. They were numbers that fit a pretty cool pattern, but they were still just numbers.

"So you're a triplet," Deirdre said. "Does that mean your mother has three kids that make a day? Are your sisters' kids also twenty-four?"

Harriet lost her smile. "Patience and Constance were born when Mama was twenty-three."

"What? How?"

"We came early. They were born at 11:55 the night before Mama's birthday. I was born at 12:05 on her twenty-fourth birthday."

"There can be only one." Deirdre grinned, but Harriet didn't share her mirth.

"Your grandmother put a lot of significance on that," her mother said. "It didn't always sit well with my sisters, even though my mother loved them just as much. Things weren't always tense between us, but when things happened that matched my mother's beliefs—our family's beliefs—in symbols, and numbers, and significance, well, Patience and Constance didn't always like the feeling that they were second-best. That they didn't matter as much."

"Did your mom make them feel that way?"

"Not on purpose. But she's enthralled when her beliefs get proven to her, when circumstances match what she's been taught, with what her mother taught her and what her mother's mother taught her. When I got pregnant with you, Meemaw told me about how Mama was worried when she was pregnant at twenty-three and when she went into labor the day before her birthday. Me coming in when she was twenty-four told her it wasn't all bunk, that these things mattered. You can imagine how ecstatic she was when I also conceived at twenty-four."

"So why did you leave? It sounds like your mom wasn't worried at all."

"No. But I was."

"Why?"

Harriet bit her lip, then said, "I was worried that the significance Mama placed on you would lead to a bad environment to grow up in, especially with my sisters."

Harriet didn't elaborate. Deirdre had already learned so much that she didn't want to push her mother for information. Still, as they rounded a clearing that opened onto barren fields, she asked, "So I guess you're not worried anymore?"

Harriet swallowed and kept her eyes forward. "Not enough to keep you from your family any longer."

Chapter 4

The open road, at last, came to a pebbled driveway. Harriet slowed the car to a stop. Both Tom and Deirdre burst out of their respective doors for the same reason: they both had to piss like racehorses.

"I'm sorry!" Tom called as he ran to a cluster of bushes a few feet from the driveway but as far from the house as possible. He unzipped his fly, then cried out in a deep pleasure that rippled across the property. Deirdre didn't have the time to be angry or even jealous of Tom answering nature's call right in the front yard. She needed to find a toilet, and she hoped to God that there was one waiting for her inside the house.

"Your family has plumbing, right?" Deirdre called as she sped towards the porch.

"Slow down!" her mother cried, huffing as she tried to catch up.

"I have to pee!"

"This is my first time back here in twenty-four years!" Harriet sped in front of Deirdre and held her shoulders to stop her from moving to the side. "Imagine if you hadn't seen me in forever, and let that determine your pace. I promise you can use the toilet as soon as you say hi to your grandmother."

Deirdre softened beneath her mother's touch, and especially under her gaze. "Okay, but let's go to the house instead of standing out here. Imagine you were pregnant with me and you'd just been in a car for a long time without stops."

"Fair." Harriet and Deirdre turned to the house. Deirdre heard Tom's footsteps catching up behind them.

Reaching the door, though, turned out to be unnecessary. An elderly woman stood on the porch, wearing a white dress and sporting a long braid that hung over her shoulder. As they neared the steps, the woman's eyes lit up. "Harriet," she said, her voice choked.

Harriet let go of Deirdre's hand as the woman—her grandmother, Yvonne, her mother's mother—hurried down the steps. They reached for one another and held each other tight. "Mama," Harriet breathed.

"It's so good to have you home," Yvonne said. "It's so good to see you again."

Deirdre looked at the door, hoping the bathroom was close to the entrance.

"Deirdre."

Deirdre looked in surprise towards Yvonne. She figured her mother had told her her name, but it still felt strange to hear it coming from a stranger's mouth, relative or not.

What unnerved Deirdre more, though, was how this stranger seemed like a mirror into her future. Where Harriet was fair and frail, Yvonne had Deirdre's dark hair and sturdy bones. Deirdre saw her nose on a stranger's face, saw the same mole on a stranger's left hand.

Yvonne reached out to her, and Deirdre felt drawn to return the hug. This woman wasn't a stranger—not anymore. She was her grandmother. She was the source of her blood and her mother's blood—

Deirdre chuckled to herself. Now she was starting to think the way her mother talked when she waxed on about her family. She had to admit, though, there was a certain inclination to do so in Yvonne's presence.

29

"It's so good to meet you," Yvonne said. "The next root of the Daylight Branch."

"Daylight Branch?" Deirdre asked.

Yvonne leaned back with a puzzled expression. "Your mother hasn't told you about the tree?"

"Deirdre really needs to use the restroom," Harriet interrupted. "We can get into that later, maybe after the party."

"And after we slice into this cake," Tom added. He held up the box, which he'd retrieved from the car on his way up the hill.

Yvonne smiled, though it lacked the gravitas of how she'd looked at Harriet and Deirdre. "You must be Deirdre's husband," she said.

"Boyfriend," Tom said as he held out his free hand for a shake.

"Yes." Yvonne kept a clipped tone as she gave Tom's hand one shake, then released him. Deirdre wondered if she was more old-fashioned about men and women "living in sin" than her mother let on.

She couldn't think about that, though. At that moment, she could only think about her bladder. "Where's the bathroom?" she asked.

"Go inside, down the hall, second door on the right before you hit the sunroom," Yvonne answered.

Deirdre handed Harriet her purse, then raced for the door before anyone else could stop her.

Chapter 5

Deirdre let out a groan so loud when she relieved herself, she was certain she'd get a dirty look from Yvonne later. At that moment though, she didn't care.

She looked at the bathroom as she did her business. Much like the house, it had a sweet farmhouse bed and breakfast feel. The bathmat and toilet lid cover were wintergreen, the curtains on the window frilly and pink. Lemon verbena soap rested on a small holder hung over the sink, which had brass knobs to turn the water on. She wondered if her relatives were cottagecore enthusiasts.

Her thoughts were interrupted by a hollow clacking, so faint it sounded like a whisper. Deirdre trained her ears on the sound, then turned to look out the window. She saw nothing but the side porch and an expanse of woods surrounding the property, with a small path cutting through the thick of it. The trees bent in a gust of wind, and the clacking grew louder.

Wooden wind chimes, Deirdre thought as she stood up. *Nice.* She flushed the toilet, and the sound of running water hushed the thwack-thwack-thwack of the chimes. She soon forgot them as she exited the bathroom.

Deirdre skidded to a stop when she saw someone waiting just outside. She looked to be her grandmother's age, perhaps a little younger. Her hair was cut in a bob and she held a lit cigarette in her hand.

"So," the woman said as she took a drag. "You must be Deirdre."

"Can you please not smoke around me?" Deirdre asked as she shielded her nose and mouth from the secondhand smoke.

The woman turned her head and blew out the smoke with a huff. "I'd smoke in there if the bathroom was free."

Deirdre stepped aside and allowed the woman to walk past her. The woman gave her a nod, then said, "I can't believe your mother brought you here."

She closed the door before Deirdre could ask her what she meant.

"Stop it!"

Deirdre jumped as footsteps thudded in her direction. She backed against the wall and saw two young girls run past her, one smiling and the other grabbing for the first one with all her might. "It's my turn!" the older one whined as she chased after the other.

"It's mine, it's mine!" the other girl said with a giggle. Deirdre's eyes widened at the sight of her holding an old wooden mallet.

"Aunt Patience said we could both practice with it!" The older one got ahold of the mallet's handle, and both girls began to tug.

"Hey, stop it," Deirdre said as she sped over to them. "You'll hurt yourselves!"

"Who're you?" the younger one asked.

"I bet that's Deirdre," the older one said with a meanness Deirdre thought she'd left behind in middle school.

"Oh, the almighty Deirdre!" The younger one held the mallet to her chest like a trophy, and the older one giggled. "The root of the Daylight Branch, the most special of them all!"

"What are you talking about?"

"Girls!"

32

Deirdre was grateful for another adult's voice. She turned and saw a woman with long, straight red hair moving towards them with an elder's disciplinary deftness. Both girls dropped their sneers and stood at attention. The woman snatched the mallet from the youngest one's hands. "If you're both going to act like brats, then neither of you get to practice."

"Yes ma'am," both said as they hung their heads.

"Thank you," Deirdre said to the woman.

The woman looked at her with a stoic iciness that almost made Deirdre miss the sneers of the children. "I assume you're Harriet's daughter?" she asked.

Deirdre nodded. The woman held out her hand. "I'm your aunt. Constance."

Deirdre shook Constance's hand. She felt less like she was meeting her aunt and more like she was greeting a potential boss at a job interview. "And these two—" Constance looked at the girls, who went from giggling at each other to standing once again at attention—"are your cousins. Faith and Felicity."

"Cousins?" These girls couldn't be older than twelve. Deirdre mentally kicked herself for expressing her disbelief out loud, but Constance only smiled. It was far from kind, but it was still better than anger.

"When you're not part of the Daylight Branch, there isn't as much of a to-do about having children in your thirties."

"Okay, what the hell is the Daylight Branch?"

"Ask your mother." She looked towards the girls. "Faith, your mom will be home soon and will want your help. Come on—both of you."

Faith and Felicity scampered off behind Constance. Felicity, the older one, stuck out her tongue at Deirdre as she passed her by.

Deirdre hung back and placed her hands over her belly. She was thinking that her doubts about meeting the rest of her family should've been heeded.

Chapter 6

Deirdre walked through the hall and heard a clamor of voices coming from a distance. She followed their sounds and ended up in a large, bright kitchen. Constance, Faith, and Felicity were there, as was the woman from the bathroom, who stubbed out her cigarette when she saw Deirdre. But she also saw Yvonne, Harriet, and Tom. Deirdre relaxed and walked straight to Tom, giving him a hug and a kiss.

"This is some house," Tom said quietly as Deirdre settled into the crook of his arm.

"Yeah." Deirdre leaned towards Tom's ear and murmured, "Though the relatives I've met haven't been nearly as charming as the décor."

Tom chuckled. "They do know this is a gender reveal party and not a baby shower, right?"

"What do you mean?"

"It's all women and girls here. Don't you have any uncles or grandfathers?"

Deirdre opened her mouth to reply, then stopped and thought. It was possible her grandfather had passed away already, and that the woman who smoked was single. But what about Faith and Felicity? Were her aunts single mothers like Harriet?

"Deirdre." Yvonne stood up, and the murmur of the family quieted around her like the end of a summer rainstorm. "Let me introduce you to everyone."

"I've met Aunt Constance," Deirdre replied. "And my cousins."

Yvonne blinked, apparently unused to being interrupted. Deirdre swallowed, then looked at her mother, hoping she hadn't embarrassed her yet again. Harriet smiled at her over her tea.

"In that case—" Yvonne waved her hand towards the woman who'd been smoking—"this is Sarah, my sister."

Sarah raised her glass in greeting. Her smirk and somewhat glassy eyes made Deirdre wonder if the brown liquid inside was something stronger than iced tea.

"Where's Patience?" Harriet asked.

"Out shopping," Yvonne replied. "We still have plenty of time before the ceremony."

Ceremony? Deirdre furrowed her brow, but before she could ask what Yvonne meant, Harriet got to her feet. "Why don't I show you around?" she offered.

"Sure," Deirdre replied, grateful to have some time away from the rest of the family. Both Deirdre and Tom walked towards her, but Harriet held up a palm. "If you don't mind, I'd like to show Deirdre around myself," she said.

"Mom, why can't he—"

"Nah, it's okay." Tom held up his hands with a smile, but Deirdre knew it wasn't totally sincere. "Mother-daughter time, right?"

"No Tom, you can—"

"You can sit with me," Sarah said to Tom as she patted Harriet's vacant chair. "You know how to play gin rummy?"

"Come on," Harriet said as she led Deirdre into the hallway. "It's a big house."

Deirdre's annoyance at Tom being excluded was outweighed by the growing relief she felt as the voices of her relatives in the kitchen grew quiet behind her and Harriet's footsteps. Harriet touched her elbow to guide her. Deirdre, in a rush of sentiment, took her mother's hand. Harriet smiled and held it as they walked.

The house seemed to grow with every corner they turned. The wallpaper was dusty rose with butter-colored stripes. Old photographs dotted the walls as they walked up the steps. Deirdre recognized Constance, Faith, and Felicity. She saw another portrait next to theirs that she assumed was Patience, since the subject was identical to Constance save for a small mole beneath her right eye.

"This is Meemaw," Harriet said, pointing at a sepia photo of a smiling older woman. "And that's your grandmother and Aunt Sarah when they were kids." Deirdre saw two portraits of young girls, both of them smiling as well.

"I didn't think Aunt Sarah could smile," Deirdre joked.

Harriet chuckled, but sadly. "She's suffered a lot of loss," she said. "Both her husband and her daughter are gone."

Deirdre immediately felt guilty for any snarky thoughts she'd had about her. She likely would've smoked and drank without a care for others too if she'd experienced that sort of loss. "I'm sorry," Deirdre said. "What happened to them?"

"They died."

"How?"

Harriet swallowed and Deirdre saw tears dot her eyes. "This is my great-grandmother," she said, pointing at another old photograph.

36

"Patience Elaine. That's who your other aunt is named after."

Deirdre studied the photograph and tucked away her curiosity for later. They reached the top of the stairs and faced a large oil painting of a middle-aged woman with a stern face. "And this is your great, great, great—" Harriet said the third "great" with an extra flourish that Deirdre couldn't help but smile at—"grandmother, Josephine. The top of the Daylight Branch."

"What on earth is the Daylight Branch?" Deirdre asked. "Yvonne—Grandma—keeps mentioning it, and so did Faith and Felicity. They didn't seem happy about it, either."

"That's probably Patience and Constance's doing," Harriet replied with a frown. "I'd hoped they'd grown out of that, but your grandmother probably didn't help things with her reverence of it."

"But what is it?"

"It's what I described to you in the car—it's us. Look." Harriet walked towards the painting of Josephine. "The Daylight Branch starts with her. Then …" Harriet turned and walked down two steps, her hand in front of her until it landed on Patience Elaine. "You have her. Then Meemaw." Harriet walked down and touched Josephine's photograph, down two steps and across from Patience Elaine. She did the same as she touched Yvonne's photo and said, "Your grandmother," moving back to the right and down two steps. Deirdre thought her mother looked like a leaf cascading down the stairs. She supposed that was intentional on the family's part in placing the portraits.

Harriet finished her descent down the stairs and pointed to herself as Deirdre followed her. "Then me," she said as she placed her hand on her heart. When Deirdre was next to her, Harriet placed her hand on Deirdre's heart. "And you."

Deirdre recalled her and her mother's conversation in the car about their ages. "So all of them were twenty-four when they had their daughters?"

"Yup." Harriet moved her hands to Deirdre's pregnant stomach. "Just like you."

"Well, we don't know yet if the baby's a girl."

Harriet swallowed and looked sad again. "No, we don't."

Deirdre was about to ask what was wrong, but the sound of the door opening stopped her. "I'm back!" the entrant called. Deirdre saw the same long red hair as Constance and the mole she'd seen in the portrait.

"Patience!" Harriet said with a smile.

"Ah, the errant root!" Patience said with a mean smile. "Back to the tree at last!"

Harriet looked down, and Deirdre narrowed her eyes. What was everyone's problem?

"You must be Deirdre," Patience said with a nod. "I'd ask you to help me with the bags, but I know you shouldn't be doing any heavy lifting."

"I'll help," Harriet said.

"No, I can do it," Deirdre said. She didn't want her mother to help anyone who was that rude to her after so many years apart.

"You've got your man here, right?" Patience said to Deirdre. "We haven't done the ceremony yet?"

"Excuse me?"

"Here." Harriet interrupted them both and took a bag from Patience. "Let's get these in the kitchen. Mama's waiting for you."

They both walked into the kitchen, while Deirdre remained in the living room. The chatter of family rose in greeting for both Patience and Harriet. Deirdre stepped away until the only sound she heard was the knocking of the wooden wind chimes she'd heard in the bathroom earlier. She leaned against the wall and swallowed back a bout of sickness she knew wasn't coming from the baby. Why couldn't they have just stayed at home?

Three Months Earlier

"Mama?"

Harriet heard her mother catch her breath over the phone. "Is that you, Harriet?"

Harriet closed her eyes and imagined her mother standing by their old landline phone in their even older kitchen, grey-green plastic against the yellow-and-rose wall. The sun would be shining through the lace curtains. Patience and Constance would be making breakfast. Aunt Sarah would be smoking and sulking over coffee.

The thought of Aunt Sarah almost made Harriet hang up the phone. But Deirdre's news that afternoon kept up Harriet's courage. Perhaps, despite the ugliness their beliefs entailed, her mother and her mother's mother, and her mother before her … perhaps they were right.

"Harriet?" Yvonne repeated.

"Yes, I'm here," Harriet said. "It's me."

"Christ, honey. To what do we owe the pleasure?"

Harriet detected iciness beneath her mother's charm. She knew just what would melt it. "It's about Deirdre," she said.

"Deirdre?"

"Your granddaughter."

"Ah. The end of the Daylight Branch, what with you uprooting her."

"She's not the end."

"What do you mean?"

"She's pregnant."

Yvonne was silent. Harriet added, "It wasn't planned. She's been seeing her boyfriend for a while now, but they weren't trying or anything—"

"It was meant to be."

"Yes." Harriet took a deep breath, then shared what made her think that maybe, perhaps, her family was onto something after all: "She's twenty-four."

Chapter 7

Tom found Deirdre in the hallway. "You coming back in here with the rest of us?" he said with a smile.

"I just need a minute," Deirdre replied. "It's been a lot."

"I understand." Tom held Deirdre's hand, and both of them took in the hallway and living room. "They definitely like the country charm," Tom observed.

"Kind of no choice when you live in the middle of nowhere."

"Are they farmers?"

"No idea."

"They decorate like they are. Look." Tom pointed at the walls. Deirdre looked and saw various gardening tools hung on the wall the same way one would display artwork or family photos. There were several spades, none of them rusted from work in the ground or being forgotten in the grass on a rainy day. There was one large pitchfork, one that gleamed as brightly as the spades. Its points made Deirdre shiver.

"These have got to be the strangest people I've ever met," Deirdre declared.

Tom laughed. "You inherit any of that strangeness?"

"God, I hope not."

"Oh come on. A little strangeness is kind of sexy." Tom pulled Deirdre close, and she giggled as he nipped at her ear.

"Well, I hope I'm not as rude as they are."

"You're the only one who isn't ignoring me, at least."

"They haven't been ignoring you."

"Please. You know it's been all about you and your mom."

"Yeah, in that except for Yvonne, they're treating us like we both have the plague."

"That's still paying attention to you.".

"Aunt Sarah paid attention to you."

Tom snorted. "Yeah, too much attention. I'm pretty sure she wasn't accidentally grazing my ass when I walked out here to find you."

"Oh for fuck's sake!" Deirdre huffed and Tom laughed. "It's not funny," she insisted, though a laugh of her own pricked at her throat. "The one person here who isn't a complete asshole to you just wants in your pants?"

"Who wouldn't want a piece of this?" Tom turned and wiggled his butt up against Deirdre. She cackled, feeling better than she had all morning.

Deirdre saw a playing card tucked in Tom's back pocket. "Were you cheating?" she asked with a smile as she pulled the card from Tom's pants.

"I'd never cheat on you," he said with a smile and a palm over his heart.

"No, silly, at cards. There's one in your pocket." Deirdre turned it over and saw a joker smiling up at her.

"Maybe Sarah gave me her number."

Deirdre didn't reply. She stared at the card. Tom's smile fell.

"What's wrong?" he asked.

Deirdre stayed focused on the card, which had a message written in crisp, hurried pen: *You + Deirdre get out now.*

"There you are!"

Deirdre cursed her mother's voice. Harriet and a team of relatives streamed into the hallway. Deirdre shoved the card in her back pocket.

"Everyone's here," Yvonne said. "Why don't we get started?"

"I'll get the cake," Tom offered. Deirdre held him back.

"You don't have to do that," she said. Whether or not the message on the card was a proper warning or more bullshit from Aunt Sarah, she didn't want Tom leaving her side.

"It's no trouble," he said.

"Cake?" Patience asked.

"Yeah, in the white box," Deirdre replied. "It'll tell us the sex of the baby."

"How does a cake do that?" Felicity asked with her face scrunched.

"The doctor told the baker, and the baker baked the cake the color that'll tell us—blue for a boy, pink for a girl."

"Doctor?" Constance sniffed. "Harriet, you really are far removed from the family."

"What, do you all blow on an egg or something?" Deirdre snapped back. Constance raised her eyebrows while Harriet dug into Deirdre's elbow with a familiar "not now" pinch. Deirdre detested her touch at the moment.

Yvonne intervened and said, "We have various means to determine a root versus a seed. Obviously, Deirdre has a different one, having grown up away from the tree."

It took every ounce of Deirdre's strength to not roll her eyes at Yvonne's continued tree talk. She half-expected her relatives to reveal themselves to be living plant creatures, feasting on chlorophyll and keeping bees in the back to help them pollinate with the outside world. But she was actually being defended, even if it was in a ridiculous way, so she kept quiet.

"We can still do the ceremony with Deirdre's cake," Yvonne declared. "Harriet, go get it. Everyone else, let's go in the living room."

Deirdre stopped Tom from moving with the group, then turned to face Harriet while holding his hand. "Let us help you, Mom."

"Come with us, Deirdre," Yvonne said. "You and Tom have a seat of honor."

Aunt Sarah's warning flashed like a strobe light in her head. "I want to help Mom," she said. *And ask her what the hell is going on.*

"It's just a cake, honey," Harriet replied with a smile. "I think my old hands can handle it."

"Let's go," Tom coaxed.

"But—"

"Deirdre." Harriet's smile disappeared in an instant. "Go."

Deirdre's blood froze at Harriet's expression. She hated that despite how old she was, her mother still had the ultimate power over her actions. She imagined it was the same for Harriet and Yvonne. Deirdre turned and walked with Tom and Yvonne into the living room.

The coffee table was covered in lace. Old wooden chairs and couches, all with cushioned seats, sat at the table's four sides, boxing it in. One couch held Constance, Faith, and Felicity; the other Patience and Sarah. Sarah gave Deirdre a sad look, and she wondered if it was because they hadn't listened to the card she'd given them. Fear began to prickle the back of Deirdre's neck like a series of keys typing one phrase over and over into her mind: *Get out, get out, get out.*

"You and Tom sit over there," Yvonne said, pointing to a loveseat at the end of the table. Deirdre took her seat, still reeling from her mother's silent reprimand. She wasn't going to cause trouble. They'd cut the cake, find out the baby's sex, then go home. Deirdre wouldn't have to talk to any of these people again. Her mother could visit on her own if she was so determined to be back.

"Incoming!" Harriet's voice rang through the living room just as Deirdre and Tom took their seats. The cake looked beautiful, sides as smooth as paper and a border of white roses all around the bottom. Even the rest of the room lost their sour expressions as Harriet set it on the table.

"What flavor is it?" Faith asked.

"Chocolate," Deirdre answered, a flash of pride breaking through her reservations. "Well, more like red velvet—or blue or pink velvet, I guess."

"Velvet sounds gross."

"It's not actually velvet, dummy," Felicity said. Faith stuck out her tongue, and Felicity looked at Constance. "Why would anyone want a pink or blue cake anyway? That sounds nasty."

"It's just for fun," Deirdre said.

"And your Aunt Harriet definitely wants a pink cake," Constance said. "Gotta keep that special line going."

"A boy will be fine too," Deirdre said.

Constance smirked, but before Deirdre could retort, Harriet said, "We'll simply have to see."

"Well, what're we waiting for?" Tom asked. "Let's dig in."

"In a moment," Yvonne said. Everyone turned their attention to her. Harriet took a seat next to Yvonne, who then stood up. She clasped her hands and looked from relative to relative, who nodded at her in turn. She settled on Deirdre and Tom. Deirdre felt her pulse quicken.

44

"We are a family of roots," Yvonne began. "It is the tree and the seed that get the attention, but it was after the loss of both that Josephine Croft realized a new way of being.

"Josephine was twenty-four years old when tragedy befell her: her beloved husband died while she was pregnant with her first child. She'd envisioned a life together, the two of them a branch on the vast family tree that made up both their lives. Each day her child grew, her heart became heavier and heavier, knowing her family was not complete. One evening late into her pregnancy, her despair reached new heights. She ran to the oak tree outside of her and her late husband's house, the home they'd been meant to grow old in together. She cried harder than she'd ever cried before. Her tears seeped into the dirt and fell in streams as long and winding as the branches of the sturdy tree."

Deirdre tried not to roll her eyes at Yvonne speaking like a minister sharing a parable. It was a gender reveal, for God's sake; not a revival.

"Her crying stopped, though, when a flash of light knocked her back. She held her pregnant belly and felt her baby kick as she looked up at the tree. The light blinded her from the branches but showed its stark, sturdy trunk—one held fast by the roots.

"She felt her water break. The stream mingled with her tears on the ground. She dropped beneath the tree and cried in pain as her daughter came into the world. Her blood seeped into the ground, nourishing the roots of the tree. Josephine knew it was not only her blood but her mother's and her mother's mother's blood too."

"Our blood is our mother's, and our mother's mother's," everyone except Deirdre and Tom recited in varying degrees of exuberance. Deirdre and Tom exchanged as quick a glance as possible to relay their shared thought of *What the fuck?*

"These mothers and daughters were the roots that kept the family strong. Seeds and pods have come and gone—"

Deirdre saw Aunt Sarah flinch and take another sip of her drink.

"Sometimes roots have come and gone—"

Harriet hung her head, and Yvonne placed her palm upon it. "But the roots never truly leave. Seeds scatter, but roots remain. And it is the roots of the Daylight Branch that keep our family centered and thriving. Josephine's oak tree still stands in our yard. Her daughter gave birth to another, twenty-four years of age. Another, and another. And now we have the latest root."

Yvonne smiled at Deirdre. Deirdre never wanted to be as far away from somewhere as she did then.

"And it's time to see if the Daylight Branch ends with a seed to scatter, or a root to keep us going strong."

Deirdre gave as best a smile as she could. Once when she was little and helping her mother garden, she'd pulled what she thought was a small earthworm from the dirt. With each tug, though, the worm revealed itself to have another fat and wriggling inch before it finally broke free, one more the size of the nightcrawlers she and her mother used to go fishing than the tiny ones she saw squirming on the sidewalk after a rainstorm. It felt like that worm was in her stomach now, getting bigger and bigger as it squirmed beneath her grandmother's gaze.

"Harriet," Yvonne said as she took a seat. "As her mother, you must hand her the blade."

"Blade?" Deirdre asked, startled. "What for?"

Harriet picked up a cake knife. "For cutting the cake, sweetie," she said.

Deirdre relaxed, embarrassed at her outburst. Still, the nagging feeling didn't leave as the ceremony continued.

"From root to root," Yvonne recited.

46

"From blood to blood," the family replied as Harriet stood. She handed the cake knife handle first to Deirdre. Deirdre took it, and her mother clasped her hand. She squeezed it and gave Deirdre a smile, one that Deirdre saw shake a little. She also thought she saw a few stray tears quiver in her eyes.

"What?" Deirdre asked.

"Just … I'm so happy for you." Harriet released Deirdre's hand and sat back down in one quick motion.

Deirdre stayed frozen with the cake knife in hand. Things weren't just weird or awkward—something was wrong. From Aunt Sarah's warning on the playing card to her mother's manner, this was more than just a strange way to do a gender reveal with an even stranger set of relatives. Something was deeply, deeply wrong.

"Go ahead, Deirdre," Yvonne said.

"What is all this?" Deirdre asked.

"The ceremony?"

"Your words. What do they all mean?"

Yvonne looked at Harriet. "Haven't you told her anything?"

Harriet flushed, and while normally Deirdre would've felt bad for putting her mother on the spot, her worry only increased. What was her mother hiding?

"You can't expect her to know everything at once," Harriet said. She nodded towards Deirdre. "Come on, let's see if it's a boy or a girl."

"This is just supposed to be a fun little gender reveal. Why are you acting so afraid?"

"You worried about being the end of the branch, Harriet?" Constance asked in a snide voice. Faith and Felicity smirked. Deirdre pursed her lips. The last thing she wanted was her atrocious aunt and cousins to get the upper hand.

"It's not the end of a branch or a root or whatever it is you all care about," Deirdre said. "Because no matter what, I'm having a baby."

47

Deirdre plunged the knife into the cake with such force, she almost smashed it. She slowed the blade's descent as she carved out a slice. Harriet fiddled with her hands, which Deirdre tried to ignore as she pulled the slice out.

Deirdre smiled as a sliver of pink slowly slid from its border of white. "It's a girl!" Deirdre said as she put the slice on a plate and lifted it for all to see.

Harriet cried out in joy, and Yvonne clasped her hands. Patience, Constance, Faith, and Felicity all smiled demurely, and Aunt Sarah raised her glass. "Congratulations, Deirdre," she said, both her tone and smile wry.

"And congratulations to Tom," Deirdre said as he stood up to give her a hug. They gave each other a kiss, and Tom touched Deirdre's belly. "I can't wait to meet her," he said, kissing Deirdre's cheek.

Harriet moved towards Deirdre, squeezing herself in between her and Tom as she pulled Deirdre into a hug. Deirdre didn't mind the broken embrace with Tom. She was too excited. A girl! A little girl she'd get to raise, a baby she could buy all those adorable dresses for that she looked at wistfully in Target.

"The Daylight Branch continues," Yvonne said, putting a pause on the celebrating. Harriet kept Deirdre cradled to her side with one arm. Yvonne walked towards Deirdre and Tom with a wide smile on her face. She placed her hand on Deirdre's stomach. Deirdre was too happy to flinch away.

"Blessed root, take hold and keep our family strong," Yvonne said.

Deirdre grinned. "She will," she replied.

Yvonne turned to Tom. "And blessed seed—"

She reached into the pocket of her dress and pulled out a garden trowel, one whose point glinted in the sunlight coming from the window.

"Thank you for your sacrifice."

Yvonne plunged the trowel into Tom's chest, blood spurting onto the white cake.

48

Chapter 8

Tom staggered back from Yvonne. She pulled the trowel from his chest and stabbed him a second time, a third.

"What are you doing?" Deirdre screamed. She lunged towards Yvonne but felt her mother yank her back. "Let me go! Tom!"

"Deirdre, stop!"

"What the fuck!"

Tom crumpled to the floor as his bleeding went from spatters to a small river staining his clothes. Deirdre yanked against her mother's hold, but Harriet pulled her back. "Deirdre, you'll hurt yourself!"

"Leave him alone!"

"You'll hurt the baby!"

Deirdre grabbed the cake knife from the table and arched her arm back to throw it. Constance grabbed her hand, and Deirdre spat in her face. "Let me go!"

Constance wiped the spit away and glared at her, then at Harriet. "How could you bring her here and not tell her what would happen?"

"Sarah, Patience, take him away!" Yvonne ordered.

"Don't touch him!" Deirdre shrieked. She wrestled against her mother and aunt's grips, watching in agony as Tom lay still and bleeding on the floor. Sarah and Patience moved quickly towards Tom. Sarah threw an apologetic glance at Deirdre as she and Patience lifted his limp body.

"You monster!" Deirdre screamed. "You're all monsters! Tom!"

"He was the seed," Yvonne said as she placed her hands on Deirdre's shoulders. "And you are the root."

"Fuck you!"

"The seeds scatter, but the roots remain."

"Fuck all of you!"

"Faith."

Deirdre twisted and wriggled, but grew weaker the longer she struggled. Faith came back with a bottle and dropper. Yvonne took it and forced the dropper into Deirdre's mouth.

"This will calm you," Yvonne said.

Deirdre began to protest but felt the words struggle and die on her tongue. She briefly caught a glimpse of the word LAUDANUM on the bottle.

"Honey," her mother said.

Deirdre's anger began to melt as Harriet wrapped her arms around her. Deirdre crumpled slowly to the floor. Harriet knelt down with her, holding her tight. She began to rock her back and forth. The world around them began to slow, slipping from Deirdre's consciousness like sand through her fingers.

"Like sands through the hourglass," Deirdre sang in a soft, dazed whisper, "these are the *Days of the Croft Family* ..."

She closed her eyes and fell away from the hell that surrounded her.

Deirdre awoke in a semi-dark room. The only light came from the afternoon sun filtering through a pink curtain. She wondered blearily how long she'd slept. As her focus sharpened, she saw that it was in an old room. Everything in it was made of rich mahogany, from the dresser to the bedside table to the bed itself. The walls had the same dusty rose and butter-colored stripes she'd seen going up the stairs with her mother earlier that day.

The events of the morning crept into her mind. Her throat began to well up with tears. Tom had been killed. She had been drugged. Her mother had brought them both here.

The fear slowly turned into anger. Harriet had to have known this was going to happen. Constance's accusation, the way Harriet held her back as Yvonne moved towards Tom, she knew. She knew, and she brought them anyway.

Deirdre got out of bed and tried the door. Locked. She jerked at it, pulling and pulling until she accepted it wouldn't budge. She gritted her teeth and banged on the door. "Let me out!" she called.

Silence greeted her. Deirdre knocked on the door again and again, pounding her fists against the wood and imagining the faces of her relatives getting beaten to a bloody pulp beneath her blows. "Let me the fuck out of here!" she screamed.

Her palms began to sting. She rested her hands on her stomach. She hoped that laudanum wouldn't cause her to miscarry, but she assumed Yvonne and the rest of the Crofts, for all their damn talk about roots, wouldn't have given her something that would've killed the baby. Her and Tom's baby—now only hers.

Tears pricked Deidre's eyes. They were supposed to be in this together. They were supposed to be a family. Yvonne's story about Josephine Croft entered her thoughts, about Josephine's pain at the loss of her husband. Josephine, though, had lost her husband. He hadn't been killed by her deranged relatives with the blessing of her mother.

Deirdre slammed her hands against the door in a thundering blow, then shouted, "I'll fucking jump out this window and end the Daylight Branch *now* if someone doesn't let me out!"

Sonora Taylor

She stood in wait. A minute later, she heard footsteps. Deirdre shook her head as she chuckled ruefully. They were so fucking predictable.

A key clicked in the door. "Honey—" her mother began as she opened it.

Deirdre slammed into her. "Let me out!"

"Deirdre!" Her mother gripped her and walked her back into the room.

"Get me out of here!"

"Calm down, you'll hurt the baby—"

"It's all about the baby, right? The only reason you came up here was because I threatened to jump!"

"What are you talking about?" Harriet locked the door behind them, and Deirdre cursed the loss of her chance to escape.

"It's what I yelled that made you come up!"

"I heard you knocking. The whole house did. When it comes to voices though, these doors are almost soundproof." Harriet knocked against it to display its sturdiness.

Deirdre crossed her arms, far from mollified. "So if I hadn't knocked, you would've left me up here to rot?"

"Don't be ridiculous. We've been checking on you on and off all afternoon."

"Oh, you're such a good mother," Deirdre said with an eyeroll. "You killed my boyfriend, but hey, you're checking up on me!"

"I didn't kill Tom."

"You brought him here. You brought *us* here—you insisted on it! You knew what was going to happen."

"I did."

Deirdre watched her mother in resigned shock. To hear her say it so plainly was almost worse than if she'd lied to her face and said she didn't know anything.

"I wouldn't have brought you, though, if I didn't think what they did was right."

Deirdre's mouth dropped a little. "How can you say that? You liked Tom."

"I did. I do. I wish things didn't have to be this way to keep the Croft family strong."

"They don't! Whatever Yvonne and her mother and mother's mother thought was necessary, it's all garbage."

"I doubted too, but then you got pregnant. Deirdre, you're pregnant at twenty-four and you're having a girl."

"That means nothing."

"It means everything. I raised you without telling you anything about numbers and meaning with my mother. You never spoke with anyone else in the family until today. When your grandmother was pregnant with three girls, only one was born on her twenty-fourth birthday. Josephine saw something powerful beneath the oak tree, and the ways we preserve her vision are keeping that strong."

"Her vision included killing the father of the child?"

"Her vision was the root, with the seeds left to scatter. The Croft women scatter the seeds to maintain the power Josephine saw in the roots."

"Mom, listen to yourself! You're talking about generational killings, fathers and husbands and boyfriends getting killed for some higher purpose. You sound insane!"

"Only because you didn't grow up with our teachings—"

"Because you didn't want me to. Why?"

Harriet's mouth twitched. Deirdre saw a flash of the mother she knew and loved, the one who occasionally got on her nerves, but at least had a modicum of sense and didn't think murder was an acceptable practice. "You left before I was born," Deirdre continued. "Why?"

"I was misguided."

"By what? It's obvious everyone here thinks super highly of Josephine's vision and murdering seeds to water the roots or whatever. Who misguided you?"

"I was my own false leader."

"You're not a stupid person, Mom. Something made you want to leave. Something was wrong. What was it?"

Harriet looked away and didn't answer. Deirdre crossed her arms. "Well, whatever it was, I know the cops won't think too highly of what's happening here."

"They leave us be."

"Not if someone reports you."

"No one's reported us. The family all believes in the vision."

"Well, I don't. I think it's a load of shit, and as soon as I leave this house—*without* you —" Harriet flinched, but Deirdre didn't care—"I'm going to the police."

"You're not leaving this house."

"Excuse me?"

"We're staying here. This is my old room, and now it's yours. I'll be moving down the hall into your grandmother's old room since she's in her mother's room."

"You can't be serious!"

"I'm not making the same mistake I made when I was pregnant with you. We're staying here."

"I'm not. Goodbye." Deirdre stormed towards the door and jiggled the handle before she remembered it was locked. "Give me the key!" she demanded.

Her mother tossed it to her, and Deirdre caught it with wide eyes. "I'm not holding you prisoner in here," her mother said. "But we're staying in this house."

Deirdre huffed as she unlocked the door, then sped out. She went downstairs and saw Yvonne, Constance, and Patience in the living room. Yvonne had changed into a fresh dress, one free of Tom's blood.

"You're awake," Yvonne said as if Deirdre had just gone down for a nap.

"Where's Mom's purse?" Deirdre asked. She wished she'd never handed her own purse to her mom, which held her phone and keys and everything she needed to leave.

"What do you need it for?" Constance asked.

"Just tell me where it is!"

"How would I know?"

"Deirdre, please calm down," Yvonne said. "We're preparing for the rest of the ceremony."

"There's more? Who else is going to get killed?"

"There's only one reaping when the root holds a root," Yvonne said without even batting an eye.

Deirdre felt a chill stab her heart. With the same calmness as Yvonne, Patience added, "We're having a bonfire. Near the oak tree."

"I'm done with whatever's next. I'm getting out of here."

"Didn't your mom drive you?" Constance asked.

Deirdre pursed her lips, and Constance smirked. Deirdre turned on her heel and walked towards the front door.

"Mom, Mom!" Faith sped past Deirdre, with Felicity not far behind her. Faith waved the hammer she'd held earlier that day. "When do we get to stop the ghosts from floating?"

Deirdre did not want to know. She opened the door.

"Where are you going?" Felicity asked.

"Away."

"You can't leave!" Faith said. "The bonfire's the best part of the ceremony! There's dancing and singing, and we scatter the seeds to keep the roots strong."

Deirdre's stomach churned at the thought of Tom's body parts, bloody and severed, being thrown into a bonfire while everyone cheered.

"How would you know?" Felicity chided Faith. "You've never been to a ceremony."

"Neither have you, but Mama talks about it all the time! I'm so glad we finally get one!"

Deirdre looked at Faith's wide, excited eyes and felt even sicker at the thought that she saw killing someone in cold blood as something both normal and thrilling. She moved past them and opened the door. She stepped onto the wraparound porch and was greeted by the sight of a large oak tree in the distance ahead of her.

So that was it. The tree where Josephine had a hallucination—*no, a* vision, Deirdre thought with sarcasm—while giving birth to her daughter, who then gave birth to another daughter, then so on and so forth until this moment. Deirdre may have found it touching if not for all the blood that had likely been spilled in the process. How had so many daughters been born through the years? Didn't the family have any sons? What happened to them? Deirdre shuddered at the thought of wailing baby boys being tossed aside or, worse, killed as violently as Tom had been. Deirdre swallowed the lump in her throat and set her chin. She had to get out, even if she walked.

"Deirdre?"

Deirdre halted at the sound of her mother's voice. She changed tack and walked to the side of the house, knowing her mother would look for her out front first. She heard the wooden wind chimes she'd heard in the bathroom clacking their hollow melody in the wind as she turned the corner.

Deirdre halted and stifled a scream.

Two skeletons blew in the breeze, their bones clacking in the wind as they hung from the porch roof. One skeleton slowly turned in Deirdre's direction, its rotten teeth in a perpetual grin.

Tom, she thought, before shaking her head. There was no way she was out long enough for the family to skin Tom and reduce him to bone. These skeletons looked old—years old at least. Deirdre wondered if they were fathers past, hung as a warning to anyone who made the mistake of getting a Croft woman pregnant. *Probably why they're in the back of the house,* she thought before spinning back around.

"There you are!"

Deirdre's heart sank as her mother turned the corner, Yvonne behind her. They smiled as they approached her. Deirdre jerked a thumb behind her. "Nice decorating," she said.

"Those are the seeds we'll scatter at the bonfire," Yvonne explained. "They've been waiting for another ceremony."

"Oh, I'm so happy to oblige." Deirdre knew that shrieking or crying wouldn't work, so the least she could do was keep some sort of dignity with unaccepting sarcasm. Still, a small part of her was relieved that bones were being scattered at the ceremony and not body parts.

"You have a lot of catching up to do," Yvonne said. "But for now, come on inside. We'll be spending enough time out here later tonight."

"We could use your help," her mother added.

Deirdre sneered. "Well, maybe if you hadn't knocked me out, I could've spent the afternoon helping you."

"How are you feeling, by the way? Do you have a headache?" Her mother walked towards her and placed a hand on her temple. Deirdre flinched back, but Harriet gripped the back of her head and pulled her close. "Stop it," Harriet whispered. "Now—or it'll be worse for everyone."

Deirdre opened her mouth to snap back, then saw Yvonne's cool stare in their direction. She remembered how casually Yvonne had mentioned the possibility of more killings—possibilities that could be threats. A small part of her—one that Deirdre wished would go away, but even with how angry she was, it remained in her heart— wondered if her mother was acting like this because she, too, was now trapped in the house with her family and their ideas.

Deirdre didn't speak, but gave a curt nod. She followed her mother and grandmother back into the house.

Twenty-four Years Earlier

Harriet crept down the darkened driveway, her purse and a small backpack full of clothes her only companions. She kept looking back at the house, waiting for one of the windows to light up and for her mother or sisters to come after her. Even when she'd made it to the main road and closer to the highway, where she could hitch a ride even further away, she saw the lights coming on in her head, one by one, her family realizing what she'd done.

She had to do it, though. The weight of her years in the house hovered above her head, waiting to crash down on her and break her legs to prevent escape. The seeds had been scattered before. The oak tree thrived with the ashes of bones that fed the roots. She was part of the Daylight Branch—her mother was right! Why else would she have floated into the womb with Constance and Patience, arriving on her mother's twenty-fourth birthday? Josephine Croft had been right, and everything they did was in good faith to her visions and prophecies.

Those actions included the scattering of pods—and after today's ceremony, for the first time, Harriet felt as if something was wrong. As the trowel plunged and the blood spattered, Harriet had a vision of the child within her suffering the same fate. It threatened to buckle her knees and gave her overwhelming grief for someone she hadn't even met yet, but was even more a part of her than her mother or her mother's mother. The child was her daughter, and she'd do anything to protect her—even if it meant leaving her mother behind.

Chapter 9

Deirdre followed her mother and grandmother into the house. She heard Patience and Constance talking and laughing in the kitchen, while Faith and Felicity squabbled over a game of cards. The gender reveal cake sat on the coffee table in the living room, its pink interior glaring at Deirdre. Tom's blood was still splattered across the top. She took a deep breath and swallowed the lump that rose in her throat. She'd get out of here somehow, but first, she had to behave.

"So what can I do to help?" Deirdre asked.

"Help with what?" Yvonne asked.

"The bonfire. Mom said you needed my help. What can I do?"

"Oh, I know that's what she said, but you're the woman of the hour. You don't have to do anything."

"I want to. Lord knows I got plenty of rest." Deirdre did her best to smile jokingly, but neither Yvonne nor Harriet were buying it. Harriet furrowed her brow, but Yvonne merely shrugged.

"I suppose you could help your aunts in the kitchen," Yvonne offered. Deirdre hoped Yvonne didn't see her blanche at the thought of being alone with them.

"Yvonne, I'm going to get more firewood," Sarah said as she walked into the room. Deirdre almost leapt with joy.

"I'll help you!" she offered. She'd get out of the house and she'd be alone with Aunt Sarah, seemingly the only person who wasn't glassy eyed with wonder at all the crazy shit this family did.

"You don't have to do that," Sarah said.

"Let me help. There's already plenty of help in the kitchen." Deirdre gave Aunt Sarah a pleading look, one she hoped would convey her desire to talk to her alone.

Sarah watched her for a moment, then nodded. "Okay."

"I don't know if Deirdre should help with that," Harriet said, and Deirdre closed her eyes. Of course, her mother would see right through her. "In her condition—"

"I'll bring the wheelbarrow," Aunt Sarah said. "And I'll do any heavy lifting. Come on, Deirdre." Aunt Sarah smiled and nodded her head towards the door. "We've got some aunt-and-niece bonding to do, right?"

Deirdre smiled as she followed Aunt Sarah out the door. "Right."

They were far from the house and past the oak tree before Deirdre dared to speak. As soon as she opened her mouth and turned her head, though, Aunt Sarah said, "You don't really just want to help me, do you?"

"I—" Deirdre lowered her voice despite their distance from the house. "I wanted to learn more about the family," she said.

Sarah set down the wheelbarrow, and Deirdre saw a wall of logs in front of them. "You stay there," Sarah said as she picked up a log. "Your mother's right, you shouldn't be doing this kind of work right now."

Deirdre had no problem with that. She stood to the side while Sarah worked. "You tried to warn me and Tom," Deirdre began.

Sarah nodded. "I guess you got the card too late."

"Why? Why are you the only one who's looking out for us?" Tears dotted Deirdre's eyes as she thought of how her mother, the person she felt the safest around, hadn't even extended her the same courtesy as a great-aunt who'd only met her that morning.

Sarah paused for a moment, holding a piece of wood in her hands. "I honestly thought your mother would too, even when she came back. That you'd leave before Yvonne could get her clutches into her baby girl again."

"You said you couldn't believe my mother brought me here. She seems pretty close with everyone, though—or wants to be."

"She's trying, at least. But I couldn't believe she brought you because you're the reason she left. She wanted to protect you."

Deirdre remembered her mother's story in the car about Patience and Constance's jealousy, and how she didn't think they'd hurt her now. Deirdre darkened as she remembered Harriet saying nothing about Tom. Still, she asked, "From Patience and Constance, right? Because they're jealous of Mom?"

Aunt Sarah snorted. "Those two and their daughters are a handful, but they're no danger to you. Just petty jealousy and sour tongues. All talk." Sarah chucked a log into the wheelbarrow, then said, "She wanted to protect you from our rituals. At least, that's what I'm assuming, considering when she left."

"Did she leave after her own ceremony? After they—" The lump in her throat reappeared at the thought of her father, likely killed in cold blood in front of Harriet. Even though she hadn't known him at all, had never heard anything about him from Harriet except that he'd died, she felt herself mourn him as if she'd just lost him. "After they killed my dad?" she said.

"No. She left after they killed Mariah, my daughter."

Deirdre recoiled as if Sarah had thrown the log at her instead of into the wheelbarrow. "They killed her?"

"Yes, along with her husband during that oh so beautiful ceremony."

"Why?"

"Because she was pregnant with a boy."

Deirdre stood frozen, unsure of what to say. All she could imagine was a man and woman at the coffee table, both being bludgeoned to death because of the baby's assumed sex and the ravings of a grieving madwoman treated by her descendants like prophecy.

"Your mother left that night," Aunt Sarah continued. "She didn't leave a note or anything, but she spent the ceremony rubbing her belly and watching with frightened eyes while she recited the usual words. The fervor she'd had before was gone."

Deirdre remembered her mother's discomfort earlier when she handed the cake knife to her. "She saw her future," Deirdre guessed.

Sarah sighed as she tossed another log into the wheelbarrow. "Maybe so."

"She brought me here anyway." Deirdre's shock dissolved into anger. "She brought me here even though I could've been having a boy."

Sarah didn't reply. She simply kept to her work.

"She knew Tom would be killed, and knew I could be." Deirdre blinked back tears. "How could she?"

"She believed through and through you were having a girl. That's what she told your grandmother when she called."

"She couldn't know for sure though."

"None of us could. For years we did the ceremony with old-fashioned ways to know if it was a boy or a girl, nothing as certain as what you have."

"So you could've just as easily killed someone carrying a girl."

"But we haven't. Your mother and your mother's mother, all of them had girls."

"But you can't know if the person is already dead. Mariah could've had a girl." Sarah flinched, but Deirdre pressed on. "How can this family accept slaughter and sacrifice?"

"When it's how you were raised, it's what you accept."

"But *you* don't accept it. I know you don't—you're the only one here who seems to have an ounce of sense. And you tried to warn us."

Sarah picked up the wheelbarrow and started back towards the oak tree. Deirdre trotted after her. "Mom said you've suffered a lot of loss. You lost your daughter. I assume you lost your husband."

"You're correct."

"Then why are you still here? Mom left, and she was part of the almighty Daylight Branch. You're just—"

Deirdre caught herself, but Sarah still turned and gave her a wry smile. "Just a root?"

"You're not 'just' anything."

"No. I'm not. And that's why I stayed." Sarah set the wheelbarrow down and pulled out a pack of cigarettes. Deirdre stepped further away, but not out of earshot.

"I'm a root, but I'm part of the whole tree—just like Yvonne, just like our mother, and just like yours," Sarah said as she lit a cigarette. Her hands and voice both shook as she blew out a plume of smoke. "At the end of the day, they're all I have."

Chapter 10

Aunt Sarah's words weighed on Deirdre's mind as they both went back to the house. It was late afternoon, and while the sun was still bright and vibrant, it dipped closer to the horizon and began to glow gold, threatening to leave like a party guest who had their coat on but still made their way from person to person for one last chat.

Deirdre assumed they wouldn't have the bonfire until it was dark. What was she going to do with all that time? There was only so much helping out she could distance herself with, especially with her mother likely knowing what she was up to.

"Wood's all set," Sarah called as they stepped inside. "And don't worry, I did all the heavy lifting."

"Thank you, Sarah," Yvonne said as she and Harriet rose from the couch. "Patience and Constance are finishing the food."

"You want to sit with us, Deirdre?" Harriet offered, gesturing towards the couch. "Mama can tell you about the bonfire, the history, and what to expect from it."

Harriet's mention of history gave Deirdre an idea. "Actually, I'd love to hear more about the 'why' of everything," she said, embellishing her interest a little bit for the sake of persuasion. She wanted to know what was going on, but not because she was especially enthusiastic about joining in on murderous rituals.

"You've got it," Yvonne said. She walked to the old bookshelf next to the grandfather clock and pulled out a large book, one with loose pages peeking out from the main ones and faded tan scuffs along the edge of the cover, suggesting many fingers had opened it. Deirdre's eyes widened. This was even better—something she could read on her own, away from everyone else.

"Could I take that up to my room? I'm kind of beat," Deirdre said, drooping her eyes for effect. "Pregnancy fatigue, you know."

"Oh, I know—I was pregnant with three, after all." Yvonne chuckled, then handed Deirdre the book. "This is everything Josephine saw, and everything we've done to see it through."

Perfect, Deirdre thought. "Thanks," she said, then exited the living room.

Deirdre found the room she woke up in before and closed the door behind her. She wished there was some sort of Do Not Disturb sign she could put on the door, but she also knew that'd be useless against her mother's key. She could only hope her grandmother and aunts would keep Harriet occupied so that Deirdre could look through the family history uninterrupted.

Deirdre sat on the bed and carefully opened the book. The spine creaked and cracked like an elderly person stretching after a nap. The first page was yellowed and featured faded but overall legible writing in ink. Next to it was a newer piece of paper with typed words—the same that were handwritten. The Croft family may have had questionable ideas, but they at least knew how to preserve them.

Deirdre recognized the first few pages from Yvonne's story, written (Deirdre presumed) in Josephine's hand. She skimmed these words as she flipped through them, not needing to relive the exact story that led to Tom being killed. She stopped, though, when she saw a page called "My Daughter and My Daughter's Daughter." Deirdre sat back and read the page in full:

Patience Elaine has a root of her own. As her belly grew, my dreams held visions of a tree crumpled beneath the weight of seeds. I realized in my waking hour that in order for a family tree to thrive, one must cast off the seeds the way trees drop their pods to scatter in the wind. Her husband Ezekiel lies in the forest and bleeds into the grass, his sacrifice nourishing our land to bring fruit to our home. Patience didn't understand at first, but when she gave birth to her own baby girl, and at the same age as I did when I gave birth to her, she realized the power our family was given from tragedy. Her daughter Joanna is a bright light in dark days. May my blood and my daughter's blood run through her and her daughter.

Deirdre took in a shaky breath as she turned the page. She saw another page in different handwriting, yet similarly titled "My Daughter and My Daughter's Daughter."

Mama Josephine was the beginning. Joanna will be happier than we ever were, as will her daughter and her daughter's daughter. Mama and I see that now. I was lost when Ezekiel was taken, but when Joanna was born and Mama's visions became clear, I realized what we'd discovered: the key to a strong foundation, one that keeps our home and our family thriving. We see it in the way we cycle, matching the hours of the day. Mama is 72, I am 48, Joanna is 24, and now Yvonne is the dawn of another day for the Crofts.

We know that trees are branches, not poles. Joanna will begin courting again to create roots from seeds. She and I feel in our bones that she'll produce another root. Mama worries we'll have seeds of our own, but it's simply not in our blood. We will produce roots, with Mama, Joanna, Yvonne, and I the roots of the Daylight Branch.

Deirdre turned the page in disbelief. All of this from one man's death ages ago. She didn't understand how they'd grown so reverential of this image of a tree, had come to accept killing people in some bizarre ritual so they could keep having girls and carry on what she presumed was Josephine's dead husband's name. She turned the page and found Joanna's entry, once again greeting her with "My Daughter and My Daughter's Daughter."

I suppose it would be more correct to say My Daughter and My Daughter's Daughters. Yvonne herself has had three! We wondered if she marked the end of the Daylight Branch, an end we know will come eventually and one Meemaw worried would be brought on by Mama having another baby. But we ended up with more roots and more branches, another way to sustain the tree without putting all of the weight on the Daylight Branch. Sarah will find seeds in due time. If she produces roots, we'll know for sure she wasn't a mistake.

With Yvonne, though, we faced a trial. She was younger than I was when she produced a root, younger than my mother and my mother's mother. We determined she was having a girl, and as she swelled, we determined she was having multiple girls. Patience and Constance came crying into the world merely as roots, but little Harriet arrived the same day as Yvonne, twenty four years later. The Daylight Branch lives on, though Mama Patience Elaine says we must be mindful of cracks in the branches.

Deirdre pressed her fingers to her temples. Her head swam with each image of the Croft women—her mother and her mother's mother, all the mothers and daughters swirling and making her dizzy the way her own growing daughter made her sick in the morning. She made herself turn the page, even though she knew it would be much closer to home. Yvonne would have written about Harriet and, possibly, her. Yvonne's entry was the last.

The Crofts have realized their mistake in expanding from the Daylight Branch, one made clear by multiple roots in my womb. If you want more roots, have them come from one seed in one womb.

This should be an entry I write after the birth of my daughter's daughter, as the entries from my mother and my mother's mother were. Harriet, though, has left our tree. No one knows where she is. She left no note, no phone number. We can't imagine she's gone far, but we also know better than to venture into town so soon after a ceremony. The police stay away so long as the seeds merely disappear.

Mariah's ceremony was yesterday. It turns out Sarah's root is not a root, but a pod—she held a seed in her womb. We scattered her as we did her seed. A consequence, surely, of straying from the Daylight Branch to continue our line. Mama was right to introduce ghost hammering to stop the malicious whispers of the spirits of seeds we have scattered.

I, myself, have two spare roots, ones who stay even though Harriet has left. They will find seeds of their own, though I can't help but wonder if they too will prove to be pods. Such is the risk to maintain the reward of our tree.

It's small comfort to know that wherever Harriet has gone, she carries a root—one that will continue the Daylight Branch. Though, if they're not with us, in our home near our tree, then this may be the end of our branch.

Deirdre expected that to be the end, but there was still another page, one in Yvonne's hand and one that even in the scribbles, Deirdre could detect her grandmother's joy:

Harriet is coming home! She shared wonderful news with me: her daughter, Deirdre, is pregnant. Deirdre is twenty-four, and if all goes as expected, as my mother and my mother's mother predicted, then she will have a girl. The Daylight Branch remains strong despite the errant roots that began in my mother's womb.

I realize now the mistakes we made. The mistake has been partially rectified with Sarah's pod. Now it is my turn. We've been given another chance. If this chance to continue the branch is true, if Deirdre holds a root in her womb, then the other roots that grafted onto us shall be pulled. Roots, after all, are below the ground, and they nourish the trunk that stays in the daylight.

Deirdre dropped the book with shaking hands. She'd seen enough with Tom and heard enough from Aunt Sarah to guess what her grandmother planned to do. She sprang up from the bed and ran to find her mother.

Chapter 11

Deirdre hurried downstairs and was struck by the quiet in the hall. There was no chatter in the kitchen, no footsteps of people preparing for the evening ahead. "Mom?" Deirdre called. "Where are you?"

Her own echo answered her. Deirdre walked through the halls. The bathroom door was open. When she walked back to the living room, everything was as it had been before, blood-spattered cake included. Where was everyone?

"Everyone's outside."

Deirdre turned and saw Felicity come in from the front hallway. She wore her perpetual frown, but at that moment, all Deirdre wanted to do was help her. She may have been one of the moodiest, most annoying girls she'd ever met, but she was a child. She didn't deserve what her grandmother had planned for her. "What are they doing out there?" Deirdre asked.

"Getting ready for you, oh brilliant Daylight Branch."

"Felicity, stop it. You need to let this go right now."

"I was supposed to go upstairs and get you. Everyone's ready."

"Where's your cousin?"

Felicity pouted. "She got to do the ghost hammering, so she's out in the woods with Aunt Patience."

Deirdre recalled Yvonne's entry. "What's the ghost hammering?"

"It's how we keep the spirits of the seeds from coming back to the house to spoil the roots. It's a big part of the ceremony."

"Felicity." Deirdre walked towards her and placed her hands on her shoulders. Felicity tried to wrench away, but Deirdre held tight. "I don't know what any of this means, but I know it's dangerous—"

"For seeds and their pods, maybe, but not for us."

"Yes, it is. Did they tell you what happened to Aunt Sarah's daughter?"

"She was a pod. She had to be scattered."

"But they didn't always do that. I've been reading the history. They keep making up new rules."

"Everything fits with Josephine's vision."

"But once it stops fitting, they make things up, and it hurts people. Felicity, your grandma's going to hurt you."

"No, she won't!" Felicity jerked free from Deirdre's grasp and glared at her. "We're all roots. Just because we're not part of your stupid branch doesn't mean we're not family."

"I know that! I know that more than any of you because I didn't grow up being brainwashed by your grandmother and the visions of a crazy old woman's grief!"

"We're not brainwashed! We're close! You and your mom don't belong here. You never should've come back!"

No, they shouldn't have; but Deirdre's pride took over. "Tell your grandma we don't belong here," Deirdre said with a sneer. "See how close you are to her then."

Felicity curled her lip but didn't reply. Tears flickered in her eyes, and Deirdre immediately regretted her words. "Felicity, I'm sorry," she said. Felicity turned towards the door, and Deirdre continued, "You need to get your cousin and you need to get out of here—"

"Because only you and Aunt Harriet belong here, right?" Felicity yanked the door open and turned back to face Deirdre with an ugly look. "Because you and your mom and Grandma and her mother's mother's mother are the only ones who count, right?"

"No—"

"Come outside. Let everyone else fall all over themselves talking about how great you are."

Felicity slammed the door behind her. Deirdre pinched her eyes shut against a blooming headache. She wasn't going to reach Felicity. She certainly wouldn't convince Patience or Constance. She may have a chance with Sarah.

But the only way she'd reach any of them was to go to the bonfire.

Chapter 12

Deirdre walked outside, then snapped her arms around her waist at the sudden rush of cold. "Jesus," she breathed, and she could practically see the curse in her breath in front of her.

"It's a lot nicer by the fire."

Deirdre looked up and saw her mother walking towards the porch with a smile.

"Mom, I need to talk to you—"

"Here." Her mother held out a hand-knit cardigan as she walked up the steps.

"Has Grandma told you anything about tonight?"

"This belonged to Josephine."

"Mom—"

"Hold out your arms."

Deirdre did as she was told. Harriet began to put the cardigan on her. "Normally this is part of the bonfire," Harriet said as she pulled the sweater tight around Deirdre's body. "To signify the passing of warmth and blood from mother to daughter. But I wanted to do it here, away from everyone."

Deirdre's eyes widened. "I thought you wanted to do everything with them now."

"We'll have time for that in the coming days. But I still wanted something like the past twenty-four years, when it was just the two of us." Harriet playfully knocked Deirdre's chin. "We'll always have that, no matter how many relatives you meet or how old you get."

Deirdre gave a small smile despite the lump rising in her throat. Maybe the mother she knew wasn't entirely lost. Maybe she could still reach her and pull her away from the monsters by the fire. Harriet had left before—maybe she would again. Even replanted, an uprooted tree never stuck to the ground the way it once did.

"Come on, honey," Harriet said as she led Deirdre by the elbow. "They're expecting us."

As Deirdre and Harriet approached the bonfire, the shadows of their family grew brighter, their shapes surrounding the bonfire in a circle. Felicity sat sulking next to Constance, while Faith and Patience sat across from them. Deirdre saw smears of blood on Faith's hands and shuddered inside her sweater. Deirdre tried to catch Felicity's eye, but Felicity made it a point to not look at her.

Yvonne stood at the head of the circle. Sarah sat to her left, and Deirdre assumed Harriet would go to her right. Harriet did just that, after kissing Deirdre's cheek and giving her elbow another squeeze.

"Welcome," Yvonne said with a smile. The shadows on her face from the flickers of the bonfire created a dance in her eyes and her grin.

Deirdre said nothing. She merely stood in place and pulled the sweater closer to her body. She could smell cinnamon and smoke coming from the wool.

"The sweater your mother gave you," Yvonne continued, "belonged to my mother and my mother's mother, and her mother's mother before her. She wore it the same night Patience Elaine and her vision were born."

Deirdre tried not to scrunch her face at the thought of any afterbirth or dried blood lingering on the sweater.

"As she gave birth to the first root of the Daylight Branch, Josephine saw a blinding light that surrounded this tree behind us. She saw seeds scattering from the branches and a beautiful crown of leaves, a family tree borne from the fire of her pain. We scatter seeds to fulfill her prophecy. We light this fire to relive it."

"Our lives are our mother's lives," the family recited.

"And our blood is our mother's blood," Yvonne said. She bent down and picked up two baskets at her feet. She handed one to Harriet and one to Aunt Sarah.

Sarah folded her hands. Yvonne beckoned her with the basket. "You must," she said.

"Please," Sarah said, a tremble in her voice.

"You know the ritual."

Sarah pursed her lips and yanked the basket from Yvonne's hands. She grabbed a fistful of whatever was in it, threw it in the fire, and thrust the basket into Patience's hands. Harriet repeated Sarah's actions, but much more slowly and deliberately, a look of reverence on her face as she tossed what appeared to be ashes into the fire.

She passed the basket to Constance. Each family member took a turn, grabbing one fistful of ashes and throwing them into the fire. When Faith and Felicity each had their turn, they walked to Deirdre with the baskets proffered, laying them at her feet.

"Remember what I said," Deirdre whispered as Felicity bent back up. Felicity scowled and left without saying a word. Still,

Deirdre thought she saw a softening in Felicity's brow compared to when she'd tried to warn her earlier.

Deirdre looked into the basket and forgot all about Felicity and Faith. There were ashes, but coarsely-ground. She could still see distinct pieces of bone sticking out of the powder.

"As the bearer of the root that continues the branch," Yvonne said, "you may now scatter the ashes of seeds and their pods into the fire, seeds that help our family grow."

Deirdre swallowed back bile, but knew by now that to protest was useless. She lifted one basket and threw its contents into the fire, wanting it to be over with as fast as possible. The flames grew and crackled with the sudden surge of food, then settled. As Deirdre picked up the second basket, she saw Sarah looking at her with tears in her eyes. *I'm sorry,* Deirdre mouthed. Sarah merely looked down, and Deirdre poured the second basket into the fire, her motions now filled with sorrow as opposed to disgust.

"The seeds have been scattered," Yvonne said.

"The seeds feed the roots," the rest of the family replied.

"The roots feed the tree," Yvonne continued.

Deirdre's relatives stood up as one, and each held a branch in their hands. "And the tree feeds our fire," they said, as they each tossed a branch into the bonfire. Sparks shot up into the sky.

A glint in the night caught Deidre's eye. Yvonne removed a trowel from her pocket. Deirdre prepared to run towards her to try and disarm her. She stopped herself, though, when she saw Yvonne pull down the collar of her shirt and run the tip of the trowel down the center of her chest, a jagged red line left in its wake.

"The mother bleeds," Yvonne recited as she swept her hand up the trickle of blood on her skin. Blood stained three of her fingers.

Harriet, Patience, and Constance moved to her side. "The daughter feeds," they recited as one. They stuck out their tongues, and Yvonne smeared her fingers across each.

Patience, Constance, and Harriet turned back to the circle and removed their own trowels from their pockets. Deirdre balked as they each walked towards their daughters. Each mother did the same as Yvonne, running the trowel down their chest and creating a streak of blood. "The mother bleeds," they said.

"Mom," Deirdre whispered. "Please don't."

"The daughter feeds." Harriet lowered her voice and said, "Stick out your tongue. It's worse if you don't."

Deirdre's shoulders slumped. This was the future she had to look forward to: increasingly disgusting and violent rituals made up by a lineage of mad women, and Deirdre having to play along because her mother knew there'd be consequences if she didn't. She'd known that when she'd run away while pregnant with Deirdre. She'd run away to protect Deirdre. And yet here she was, back again, pulled in by some sort of love for this family and some sort of belief in numerical coincidences.

Deirdre stuck out her tongue in resignation. Harriet ran a clean finger over Deirdre's tongue, then brushed her fingers in Deirdre's hair while cupping her cheek, cleaning off the blood. She winked, then kissed her cheek and whispered, "All in good time."

Deirdre watched with a glimmer of hope as Harriet returned to Yvonne's side. Maybe she wasn't as far gone as she'd feared.

1997

"It's a girl!"

Harriet cried with joy as the pendulum swung in the correct direction over her pregnant belly. Yvonne seemed almost happier than Harriet. She hugged her close, and happy tears wet Harriet's shoulder. "The branch continues," she whispered. "We've rectified the mistake that Meemaw made."

"What mistake?" Harriet asked. Everything was such a blur that she almost didn't notice Meemaw Joanna begin her thanks to Brian for his sacrifice of seed. He cried in terror as the trowel plunged into his chest. He called Harriet's name, but she looked instead at her mother. "What do you mean?" she asked.

"Come with me." Yvonne grabbed a dusty book from the bookshelf, then led Harriet upstairs to Harriet's room. Brian's screams from downstairs were shut out entirely when Yvonne closed the door. She and Harriet sat on the bed, the white and pink quilt still making Harriet curl her upper lip at how childish it looked.

"This is the book we started after Josephine gave birth to Patience Elaine. It's a chronicle of the Daylight Branch and the fulfillment of Josephine's vision. Each mother writes in it when her daughter becomes a mother."

Harriet gently turned the pages, careful not to tear them, for they were delicate with age. "I'll be writing my entry when your little girl is born," Yvonne said with a smile. "Just like Meemaw Joanna wrote hers when I was born."

"And Aunt Sarah, right?"

Yvonne furrowed her brow. "She's the mistake you corrected, honey."

"Aunt Sarah isn't a mistake. She's a root."

Yvonne folded her hands and took a deep breath. "Things stopped going to plan once she was born. I met my seed earlier than I should have. I became pregnant too young, younger than my mother and my mother's mother."

"But you said I was—"

"The Daylight Branch, yes, because of grace. Because you floated in to be born with your sisters, roots that grew in my womb all at once. The only way roots should grow, at least according to Josephine's vision. And even they risked ending the Daylight Branch, being born before I turned twenty-four." Yvonne cupped Harriet's cheek and gave her the smile Harriet loved so much, the one she knew held pride in her daughter. "But you waited just long enough and kept our branch going strong. We were given another chance, one we won't squander."

"I promise not to squander it," Harriet said. "I'm having a girl. It's continuing."

"Yes it is, and we're all so happy."

Harriet had seen Patience and Constance's expressions and knew that was a lie. Still, she'd done it: she was having a girl, and her mother and her mother's mother would live on through her daughter and, hopefully, her daughter's daughter. The Daylight Branch would continue, even with the extra roots added on through her sisters and through Aunt Sarah.

Harriet felt a twinge of pity for Aunt Sarah. Aunt Sarah was always kind to her and her sisters. She made excellent cornbread and gave the most interesting lessons during their school time. She wished she wasn't treated like an afterthought just because she was her mother's sister. And Sarah's daughter, Mariah, was much nicer to Harriet than either Constance or Patience. Mariah had just announced her own pregnancy a month ago, and it was met with considerably less excitement than Harriet's own announcement.

"Maybe Mariah will have a girl," Harriet offered. "Maybe she'll start a new branch off of the Daylight Branch. Maybe she and Aunt Sarah aren't mistakes, but extensions."

Yvonne squeezed Harriet's hand. "We'll see." But Yvonne's expression said she didn't have much hope for Mariah's prospects— or, worse, that she wouldn't care even if she did have a girl. Harriet felt a twinge of annoyance. What made them so special? Why was

Yvonne so worried about the other mother's wombs when she was continuing the Daylight Branch? They were all family—wasn't that what mattered?

Yvonne patted Harriet's knee. "Let's go back downstairs with everyone else," she said. "We need to get ready for the bonfire."

Harriet rose to join her. They were her family, and even when Harriet didn't understand them or why they thought the way they did, she knew they were bonded by blood, blood that flowed from mother to daughter and kept the line strong. Still, Harriet couldn't help but feel the beginnings of a nagging doubt growing alongside the daughter within her.

Chapter 13

The fire crackled as Harriet, Patience, and Constance returned to their places. They each set their trowels on the ground at Yvonne's feet.

"Deirdre," Yvonne called. She beckoned with her hand. "Come."

Sarah moved to the side and stood with Constance and Felicity. Deirdre walked by them and whispered as quickly as she passed, "Get out now." She wasn't sure if Sarah heard, but she had to at least try. As she stood by Yvonne's side, she saw Sarah give her a curious glance but otherwise stayed put. *Leave*, she begged her aunts and cousins in a loud mental voice, one she hoped they'd somehow hear. *Run!*

"The Daylight Branch stands at the top of the tree," Yvonne said. She held her hands in front of Deirdre and Harriet each as if she were in prayer. "The Daylight Branch—"

"Holds other branches," Sarah recited. Deirdre watched in curiosity as she, Patience, and Constance glided to the other side of the fire, stopping at an angle away from Harriet. Sarah, Patience, and Constance recited together, "And the branches—"

"Are held by the roots," Faith and Felicity recited in unison. They stayed on their side of the fire but moved in a similar glide to another angle. Their stances reminded Deirdre of the pictures arranged on the stairwell, an image of leaves falling from the head of a tree. Faith and Felicity clasped hands. Sarah, Patience, and

Constance followed suit. All lifted their arms as if they were about to dance. They all looked towards the three of them. Harriet reached for her mother's hand. Deirdre was about to do the same until Yvonne pushed Harriet's hand away. The wounded look in Harriet's eyes nearly broke Deirdre's heart.

Yvonne looked at Deirdre. A sudden knot formed and unspooled in Deirdre's stomach, leaving threads of cold fear knitting through her skin. She looked at her mother, who stared at Yvonne with fear in her own eyes. She had no idea what Yvonne was going to say. None of them knew. They were all at Yvonne's mercy.

"Dierdre, go stand with Faith and Felicity." Yvonne turned to Harriet. "Harriet, go stand with Patience and Constance. And Sarah, come stand with me."

Deirdre and Harriet hesitated, as did Sarah. Yvonne crossed her arms, but in a way that looked holy as opposed to demanding. "I've had a vision," she said. "One that will change our dance."

Sarah and Harriet nodded and turned to move. Deirdre was slower to leave but moved when she considered how far away Faith and Felicity were from Yvonne and anything she might do. Deirdre took her place beside her cousins. Felicity made it a point to step several inches away from Deirdre. Faith looked confused, but still followed her sisters' motions.

Yvonne uncrossed her arms and spread them wide. The fire let out a pop as she did so, creating an effect that even Deidre found spellbinding. "Look at our tree," Yvonne said. "Josephine's vision continues, the Daylight Branch bringing fire to the ground, the seeds scattered to strengthen our light and continue the flow of our mother's blood and our mother's mother's blood. As the blood flows down, it crisscrosses like a leaf in the fall, moving into the roots to nourish our line and continue to replenish the tree.

"But as our tree has grown, the path has become too winding. It's created roots above the ground, errant roots that divert the blood and threaten to diminish our fire. My mother began this trend. My womb continued it, a signal that she'd been mistaken. If we're to have multiple roots, they must come from one seed.

"But even multiple roots weigh heavy, diverting the blood away from the line. We began producing pods instead of roots. A root of the Daylight Branch left the tree. Things have been rectified, but we cannot risk the ultimate scattering of roots that will turn us all to ash."

As Yvonne spoke, nervous glances began to pass across the family. Still, no one moved.

"There is a purpose for multiple roots," Yvonne said. She picked up a leather satchel next to her. "We usually dance with the scythe to celebrate the scattering of seeds." She lifted a gleaming blade from the satchel. It caught every spark and beam of light from the fire, shining as brightly as the moon. "But tonight, we harvest with the scythe to send the errant roots where they can best nourish the tree: underground."

Yvonne swiveled, then slashed the blade across Sarah's throat.

Chapter 14

A chorus of gasps sounded around the fire as Sarah collapsed to her knees. "Yvonne," she began, her words a curdled gurgle in her throat.

Yvonne ignored her, slashing Sarah once, twice, three times more until she lay limp on the ground, her blood soaking the grass. Yvonne smiled as she held up the blade, blood spattered over her dress and her chin. "Her blood flows as Josephine's flowed when she birthed the first root," she said.

Deirdre felt the scream in her throat, even though she'd suspected this was coming the moment she read Yvonne's entry in the family journal. What kept it caught, as well as her feet planted in the ground, was the stillness of her aunts and her cousins. They looked horrified, but they didn't scream. They didn't move. Weren't they going to run? Didn't they know this was also going to happen to them?

Deirdre turned and looked at Faith and Felicity. Faith hid behind her cousin, and Felicity looked horrified. "Felicity," Deirdre hissed. "Run!"

"Harriet," Yvonne said. She walked towards Harriet and held out the blade to her. "You must prune the errant roots from your branch."

Patience and Constance huddled next to each other, yet still stayed put. So many years watching others be sacrificed, and now they couldn't think to save themselves.

Harriet held the blade but didn't wield it. "Mama," she stammered. "They're my sisters."

Yvonne frowned. "They're the consequence of straying from Josephine's vision. We must scatter them as we scatter seeds and pods, as we'll scatter my own sister."

"Josephine never said that—"

"As the line grows, so do the rituals. We knew this when Mariah was a pod, which we'd never had before. We're breaking thanks to all the errant roots. We need to correct it."

"We're not errant roots, Mama," Constance snapped. "*She* is!" She pointed at Harriet. "She's not identical to us, she floated into the womb! She left us because she never belonged!"

"What?" Harriet's eyes widened as much as Deirdre had ever seen them.

"You ruined the line! Because *you're* the errant root!" Constance yanked the blade from Harriet's hand and slashed her across the chest. Harriet cried out in pain and fell to the ground. Constance knelt and struck her shoulder, blood splattering across her face.

"Mom!" Deirdre screamed. She began to run towards her, but Yvonne was faster. She wrested the scythe from Constance and swept the blade across her throat. Constance fell to the ground, cupping her neck as her fingers went from white to crimson in less than a second. Patience screamed and turned to run, but Yvonne caught her across her Achilles tendons. Patience's cries rang through the trees like the wails of a thousand lost souls. Yvonne stood over both of her fallen daughters, slashing them until the only screams left were those of Faith and Felicity as they watched their mothers die.

Harriet lay curled into herself, unmoving. Tears streamed down Deirdre's cheeks. "Mom," she said, moving closer.

Yvonne blocked her path to her mother. Her face, cardigan, and hair were matted with blood. Faith wailed behind Deirdre as Felicity shushed her. Deirdre stood stone-still, as tall as she could, locking eyes with a grandmother she'd never cared to meet in the first place. Deirdre crossed her arms. "I'm not killing anyone," she said.

"Of course you aren't," Yvonne replied. Her stare was as cold and black as the night sky, with only the flames of the bonfire reflected in her irises. "It was you who made your mother leave us. It was you that made your aunts hate your mother, and your returning that brought all of this upon us." She used the hem of her cardigan to clean the blade. "You're the errant root, Deirdre—and you will be removed."

Yvonne lifted the blade. Deirdre jumped back, but Yvonne suddenly faltered. The scythe fell out of her hand as she lost her balance, teetering towards the ground.

Deirdre saw Harriet on her stomach next to Yvonne, head up and eyes alert with anger. Harriet let go of Yvonne's skirt, then grabbed the scythe and hacked the back of Yvonne's shins. Yvonne howled with pain. Harriet struggled to her knees, her sweater soaked with blood from the wound in her stomach. "No more," she growled.

"Baby," Yvonne pleaded.

"This ends with you!" Harriet used every ounce of strength she had left to shove Yvonne backward into the fire. Yvonne screamed and cried as the fire consumed her, sparks flying into the night. Soon the crackles of the fire drowned out Yvonne's yelling, and her body became a red, bloody mass engulfed by the flames.

Chapter 15

Harriet collapsed onto her stomach as Yvonne burned beside her. She rolled onto her back and coughed. Blood sputtered over her lips.

"Mom!" Deirdre yelled as she ran towards her. As she knelt beside her mother, she looked up to check on Faith and Felicity. Both were gone. They must've run away during Yvonne's final moments, or maybe when Yvonne had advanced on her with the blade.

"Baby."

Deirdre looked back down at her mother as Harriet reached a weak hand towards her. All thoughts of her cousins flew out of her head. Deirdre knelt down and took Harriet's hand.

Harriet coughed again. More blood spilled onto the grass. Deirdre sat cross-legged and gently lifted her mother's head. Harriet lay on her lap as her breathing grew ragged. Deirdre remembered all the sick days Harriet had done the same for her. Deirdre's tears began to mix with Harriet's blood.

"I'm sorry," Harriet whispered. "We never should've come here."

"Why? Why did you—"

"I thought they'd never hurt you. I thought the visions were real when you got pregnant, that Mama and Meemaw were right."

"No. Why did you stop Yvonne?"

Harriet looked up and locked eyes with Deirdre. "You're more important to me than any vision. It's why I left. I saw—" Harriet succumbed to a coughing attack, and Deirdre held her closer. Harriet cleared her throat, then continued, "I saw them kill Mariah. I didn't want them to kill you."

Despite Harriet dying in her arms, Deirdre stiffened at the memory of Harriet clasping her hand in fear before they found out she was having a girl. "What if I'd been a pod?" she asked. "What if I was having a boy?"

"I wouldn't have let anyone touch you." Harriet grabbed Deirdre's hand and squeezed it tight, tighter than she'd ever held it. "You mean more to me. You've always meant the most to me."

"And you mean the most to me, Mom."

"I can't mean the most to you anymore, baby." Harriet released Deirdre's hand and placed it on Deirdre's stomach. "She should."

Deirdre sobbed. "No, Mom, no—"

"She has your blood and my blood. By taking care of her, you'll be taking care of me. Just like you're doing now."

Harriet coughed again, and Deirdre held Harriet's cheek. "I can get help," Deirdre said. "You're still speaking, you still have some life in you."

Harriet took Deirdre's hand again and squeezed it, more gently this time, but with more love than Deirdre had ever felt before. "I love you."

Deirdre spoke despite how choked her throat had become. "I love you too, Mom." And it was the truth. In spite of everything that had happened, in spite of the family Harriet had brought into Deirdre's life, she loved her.

Harriet's breathing grew still. The bonfire crackled beside her, the flame slowly dying.

Chapter 16

Deirdre walked towards the house in a daze. The fire burned behind her, the bodies of her relatives scattered around it in a danceless circle. She heard the crackle but paid it no mind. She only thought of getting inside. A phone was inside. Bodies weren't inside.

The door closed behind her. A heavy shroud of silence draped over her like an old sweater. Deirdre shivered at the thought of Josephine's sweater on her body, then closed her eyes at the memory of Harriet lovingly pulling it close over Deirdre's chest. Warm tears tapped her eyelids, gently trying to get her to open them.

Deirdre swallowed back her tears as she opened her eyes. She wondered if her cousins were hiding in the darkness. "Faith?" she called in a shaky voice that barely traveled to the kitchen, let alone through the full house. "Felicity?"

Deirdre began to look for them, then stopped with a shuddering gasp in the living room. The gender reveal cake sat in the moonlight coming through the windows. That wretched cake still had splatters of Tom's blood on it. Everything had been left as it was—except for a napkin against the side of it. It looked like it'd been tossed and only stood up because it stuck to the icing. There was a hurried scrawl across it, but Deirdre could still make it out:

Thank you.
Please don't look for us.
—Felicity

They were gone. They'd done what Harriet had done twenty-four years ago, what Sarah should've done, and what Deirdre should've tried harder to do once Sarah had warned her. Seeds of doubt ran wild through this purportedly blessed branch, and yet barely anyone had done anything to stop what had happened for generations—not even Deirdre, until it was too late. And even then, she knew it was because her mother had raised her away from the family. Harriet had never taught Deirdre that ritual sacrifice was normal, that murder was necessary to keep the family together. What would Faith and Felicity do, out there on their own?

Deirdre left the living room. After a slow but thankfully brief search, she found her mother's purse in the kitchen. It held Deirdre's small clutch, the car keys she'd wanted so desperately earlier that day, her mother's cell phone, and her own. Neither one had a signal. "Of course," Deirdre muttered. She knew, though, that there was a landline. She walked to the phone and dialed 9-1-1.

"Hello, what's your emergency?" said a vaguely disinterested male voice. Deirdre could picture a tired police chief at his desk, upset that his crossword puzzle had been interrupted.

"My name is Deirdre," she said in as steady of a voice as she could. "Several of my—my family's been killed."

The man's voice picked up. "Is there an intruder? Are they still there?"

"No."

"Are you in danger?"

90

"No, I'm—it was done by the family. By my grandmother."

"Oh Christ," the cop sighed, then caught himself. "Sorry. Is she still there?"

"No, she's dead. Everyone's dead."

"Where are you?"

"I'm …" Deirdre realized she didn't know the street they were on or even the house number. Her mother hadn't used the GPS.

"Ma'am, are you still there?"

"Yes. I don't know the address. It's an old farmhouse. It was owned by Yvonne Croft."

"Croft?"

"Yes. I'm Deirdre Croft, her granddaughter."

"The Crofts—" The officer stopped himself abruptly, but Deirdre still heard the change in tone. More so, she felt a shift between them on the phone, one she hoped she was only imagining.

"Can someone please come?" she continued. "I'm alone and—"

"We'll find you, Deirdre." Formal. No longer shocked.

"I can go outside and find the number, the street—"

"Just stay inside and stay safe. Can you do that?"

"Y-yes."

"Okay. Stay there. We'll be there shortly." The officer hung up without saying goodbye. Deirdre walked back to the living room. She sat and tried not to stare at the cake. She waited for a police officer she knew would never come. A family with such a rich and deadly history surely knew that the best way to keep the silence of the authorities was to buy it.

Time passed. Deirdre sat, staring at the empty house before her. She kept her back to the stairs that were lined with portraits. The last thing she wanted was to look at Josephine in the eye, at any of them, really. The only one she wanted to see was the one whose portrait wasn't on the wall.

Deirdre was, of course, still angry that Harriet brought her and Tom here in the first place. But in the faintest of ways, she could see what her mother and her mother's mother wished for. They'd wanted to keep the family bond, the passage of blood from one woman to the next. To keep their hearts from breaking by only giving them to each other, with everyone else left behind or driven away by the knife. It wasn't right, but, as Deirdre sat in a home with no one asking her what had happened, no one there to wonder what she'd been thinking or why she hadn't done more, she could see the appeal of going along with what the family said.

But with each passing year, the family said to kill more—including their own. Deirdre shuddered as she remembered Yvonne gladly handing her the family's book. She'd thought nothing of the fact that Deirdre would see the fate that lay in store for her aunts and her cousins. She'd thought she'd go along with it. Had Yvonne thought the same of Harriet? Probably not—her mother had seemed genuinely shocked when Yvonne instructed her to kill her sisters. And even if she'd known, maybe she'd faltered when the moment came, unable to face it once it was happening—much like when she left after Mariah had been killed in cold blood because yet another rule had been added to Josephine's original vision.

Deirdre would never know, though, because her mother was dead.

Deirdre buckled over and began to sob. Her cries rang through the house and tore through the walls. Tom being gone hurt her deeply, and she'd mourn him for the rest of her life. But her mother being gone was like a piece of herself being gone, one that burned to ash in the bonfire, that seeped into the dirt with her mother's blood to freeze in the winter and feed the flowers and grass in the summer. To feed that fucking tree that her grandmother and her grandmother's grandmother loved so fucking much that they'd murder their own roots to keep it strong.

As Deirdre's sobs calmed into hiccups, she felt a wave of heartburn roil up her chest. She was still pregnant, after all. Deirdre breathed slowly to stop the hiccups, then placed her palms over her belly. She was pregnant. She had a daughter on the way. A daughter she would love, a daughter that held what was left of Tom. A daughter that held her blood and her mother's blood. It was a cold comfort, but one that Deirdre understood would motivate someone like Josephine when she'd cried beneath the oak tree and thought that all was lost.

Deirdre wasn't Josephine's daughter—she was Harriet's. Harriet had the sense to leave this place, to get as far away as possible in order to protect her child. She'd been pulled back. She'd risked her own life and her daughter's to see her mother again. Deirdre understood how Harriet felt, now that she was here without a mother she had any hope of ever seeing again.

While Deirdre was Harriet's daughter, she wasn't Harriet. She got to her feet, sighed, and picked up her mother's purse. She held her head high as she walked through the door. She'd follow in her mother's footsteps—but unlike her mother, she'd never return. She had her daughter and her daughter's daughter to think of.

Afterword

They say you can't go home again. That's not true. You can, but you may not like what you find there, and instead have the reasons why you left return with a singing bitterness that will last, well...until the next time nostalgia visits.

But what happens when you discover family and traditions that you never knew about, that have been hidden from you your entire life? There is always a sinister feeling that creeps in when a group of heretofore unknown family members is suddenly thrust upon you. Even more so when you're in a vulnerable position.

Add to that vulnerability, the realization that a trusted person's actions have turned them into someone you no longer know or recognize. Then, the knowledge of how alone you truly are slowly dawns. You are alone in the midst of a sea of people. Their features look so familiar you recognize them in yourself. They are actively out to harm you.

But roots run deep, hearkening back to an ancestor whose pain-induced vision created the mold that the entire family had adhered to for generations. Then in 1997, Harriet breaks free. No one pursues, tries to track down the prodigal daughter and return her to the fold.

Yet, she returns on her own, twenty-four years later, clinging to her own daughter who is carrying the future.

Scatter the seeds. Secure the ghost.

It's the ultimate betrayal.

Deirdre discovers this during the events of *Errant Roots.* Unmoored due to an unplanned pregnancy, she turns to her mother, Harriet, for support. Unaware of what awaits her, Dierdre and her baby daddy are dragged to an impromptu family reunion at Harriet's remote ancestral home. There, Dierdre's previously reliable mother changes, helping facilitate her own daughter's isolation, entrapment, and the murder of the baby's father.

It's said that the most difficult thing in the world is to change your position in your family's hierarchy. And Dierdre's mother suffers from that. Even though she is a mother herself and fully knowledgeable of what her family's homicidal legacy is, Harriet falls back into her old ways, and back into step with her former place in the family.

Funerals and births, while on opposite sides of our existence spectrum, are the two main reasons many families come together. Births are generally a time of celebration, but it is also a time of pain and reflection. Family members can feel they have the right to swoop in and take over responsibility for a new life, often leaving the expectant mother feeling without a voice, without control over their own body.

The roots of your family tree can run deep, but they can also become twisted, spreading a seeping rot that will eventually affect everything.

Deirdre's anxiety grows the longer she is around her strange family. Not only does she feel out of place, she is clearly the only one not in on the long-held family secrets. There are whispers, glances, talk about her importance to the family because she is *the branch* or some such she doesn't understand. Even with this importance, Dierdre isn't spared the snide comments from those jealous of her standing in the hierarchy. She wants nothing more than to go home and for everything to go back to the way it was before she announced her pregnancy.

Soon, it's all too apparent that is impossible. Her baby's father is dead, her mother is no longer the person she remembers and trusts, and a ritual is once again beginning under the light of a bonfire and the blaze of madness in her grandmother's eyes. Dierdre witnesses how easy it is for a matriarch to become a despot.

At the end of that trial by fire, Deirdre and her unborn daughter are the only ones left on the family land. It's then Deirde looks out on all that she came from, all that came before her, then gets up and walks away.

At the end, it turns out Deirde wasn't the branch. She was the seed, and she's letting the winds of change take her elsewhere, hopefully to a place where she can tend and nurture herself and her daughter. And finally, put down her own stronger, healthier roots.

—Eden Royce
Author of *Hollow Tongue*

About the Author

Sonora Taylor is the award-winning author of several books and short stories. Her books include *Someone to Share My Nightmares: Stories, Recreational Panic: Stories, Seeing Things, Little Paranoias: Stories, Without Condition, The Crow's Gift and Other Tales*, and *Wither and Other Stories*. She also co-edited *Diet Riot: A Fatterpunk Anthology* with Nico Bell. Her short stories have been published by Rooster Republic Press, Kandisha Press, Camden Park Press, Burial Day Press, Cemetery Gates Media, Tales to Terrify, Sirens Call Publications, Ghost Orchid Press, and others.

Her short stories and books frequently appear on "Best of the Year" lists. In 2020, she won two Ladies of Horror Fiction Awards: one for Best Novel (*Without Condition*) and one for Best Short Story Collection (*Little Paranoias: Stories*). In 2022, her short story, "Eat Your Colors," was selected by Tenebrous Press to appear in *Brave New Weird: The Best New Weird Horror Vol. 1*.

For two years, she co-managed Fright Girl Summer, an online book festival highlighting marginalized authors, with V. Castro. She is an active member of the Horror Writers Association and serves on the board of directors of Scares That Care.

She lives in Arlington, Virginia, with her husband and a rescue dog.

Content Warnings

The following content included in Errant Roots may be triggering to some individuals:

- Child endangerment
- Murder of a pregnant woman (spoken of/remembered, not shown)
- A character wonders if babies have been murdered and briefly imagines it happening
- Multiple murders by blade, including throat slashing
- Blood
- Burning alive
- Cults/cult-like behavior
- Matricide (killing one's mother)
- Loss of one's mother
- A character is drugged against her will
- Family trauma

www.ingramcontent.com/pod-product-compliance
Lightning Source LLC
Chambersburg PA
CBHW052013240626
47153CB00008B/2861